Prol

Big waves gushed throughout the narrow river, sending the small wolf off balance. He couldn't see over the water. Every time he tried to stand up to get out, a huge ripple would crash down on him, pushing him back under the murky water. He flapped his paws, up and down, trying to paddle his way to the edge of the stream. But he couldn't. Only critters scurrying among the forest could hear the small wolf's desperate cries. At least, that's what the pup thought.

A large, gentle omega wolf was wandering around the forest. The wolves in his pack had kicked him out; for he was the lowest rank in the pack, and didn't ever have anything to do. The wolf trudged along the squishy dirt ground, thinking about what to do next. He had lots of wounds, stinging his back and legs and face.

He heard a yowl. The gentle wolf felt a shiver go down his spine. He trotted swiftly, ignoring the distant wails. He began jogging, trying hard to not pay attention to the noises of the forest around him. He ran across the undergrowth, panting wildly.

He skidded to a halt when he reached the narrow river. The water was wild, crashing and splashing in every direction. The wolf knew this was where he heard the wails. Although he was trying to ignore them, he couldn't for long.

A loud cry echoed from the water, and the large wolf stepped back. He was correct, the screeching was coming from the stream. He was about to keep running. The screams frightened him. Suddenly, a small paw flew out of the water, desperate gurgles from under it. The large, gentle wolf launched in, taking the small wolf by the scruff carefully.

The small wolf was still crying while the large wolf waded through the crashing water. Jumping out of the river, he shook off his wet fur. The wolf stared down at the pup, who stopped yelling but was whimpering and shivering. He tried to calm the pup down, licking it with his huge warm tongue.

The pup's glittering purple and yellow eyes opened as he finally calmed down. He stood up, shaking his short pelt. He blinked at the big, gentle wolf, and smiled a little bit. "Thank you for saving me…" said the pup's small, piercing voice. "I… I don't think I would've been able to do it myself."

The gentle wolf blinked in surprise. Not all pups could talk, and when they could talk, they weren't as polite as this little wolf. At least, in his pack they weren't.

"No problem, pup… how did you fall in, anyway? W-well, if you don't want to share it with me, that's okay too…"

"No, no, I'll tell you. I was looking for a place to stay for the night. I don't have any family members or friends to stay with, so I'm all alone. Anyway, I was walking next to the stream, hoping to catch any fish. I was starved. I finally caught one, and was chomping it up, when suddenly something big... really big... rammed into me. I stumbled into the river, and the cold water startled me, and I was paralyzed for about ten seconds. The thing that pushed me in stared into the water. It... it didn't try to help me. It just stared."

The pup took a deep breath and quickly rubbed his face with his paw.

"It had green eyes... no, one green eye and a blue eye. That's it. The creature looked at me for fifteen seconds and then stalked away and didn't look back. I think it was a wolf, but it was so big... so, so big..."

The pups eyes glimmered, and the larger wolf could see he was about to start crying. He licked the pups head and whispered, "It's okay... you don't have to tell me it. I can tell it's upsetting you. It's okay, you're okay now." The pup looked up at the big, gentle wolf. "Do you have a pack?" The former omega blinked. "Well, I used to. B-but, I got kicked out... today." The pup blinked surprisedly.

"Oh. Sorry that happened... HEY! Maybe you and I could live together!"

The gentle wolf blinked. 'Living with a pup is better than living alone...' he thought. "Okay. I'm Echo." He said. The pup smiled. "I'm Willow."

Chapter 1

Rona walked across the rock path leading to her home. She crouched down in her flower bed. The town was great; It had over fifteen wolves. Standard towns only have fifteen. The neighborhood wasn't really a neighborhood, though. It was just a path with twenty paths jutting out of the sides, leading to beds.

The wolves that lived in the town all greet each other every morning, and then do their own things. They hunt, search for important things, and build more beds for pregnant female wolves' future pups. They all care for each other, but not so much that they spend as much time with each other as possible.

Rona was the leader of the pack, the ruler, the alpha. She cared for everyone in the pack, even the useless, lazy omegas.

Well, almost everyone. One wolf was horrible. A nightmare. A mistake. This was Echo, a big, ugly wolf that didn't ever move from his bed. Rona and the wolves got so sick of him sitting around, they replaced his flower bed with sharp rocks and moved it a mile away from the town.

Although, Echo didn't care. He wasn't like others. He was odd.

"He doesn't want to be a wolf," Rona heard a Zeta female wolf saying to an Iota male. "He doesn't want to be here."

Rona didn't think that. She thought Echo did it to be a snob. So did her Beta, Delta, and Gamma, Moose, Grayson, and Barn. They all gossiped together about how dumb he was, and what time they should kick him out.

But they never did.

"We should wait 'till he gets so mad he leaves on his own," said Barn, pawing at the ground excitedly. Grayson padded around nervously in front of Rona while she sat in her bed.

"But guys," Grayson started, rubbing his paws together like he was cold. "Echo will never leave! I know what he's planning! I... I know what he's gonna do, and you'll be shocked when you find out what it is!"

Moose smiled at him and laughed. "What's so shocking? He can't even talk, I bet. He's an IDIOT! I assume he's too fat to even stand up."

Grayson grumbled towards Moose, but then continued nervously rubbing his paws together. "He's gonna kill us all! He's gonna kill us!!!

Rona burst out laughing. "I'd like to see him TRY!"

Grayson shook his head. "He wants to take over the pack, I just know it. I can see it in his eyes."

"I'm gonna drive him out," Rona announced. "C'mon guys, come claw him with me." The 3 wolves followed Rona across the forest, their paws scraping against the dry, dirt ground, vibrating the undergrowth.

When they reached Echo's sharp rock bed, he was sitting in front of it on the ground. Rona was disappointed he was in front of it, instead of hurting himself on top of the bed. "Hello, Rona. Oh, and hi, Grayson, Moose, and… B-bubby, is it?" Barn growled and lunged at him, scratching and biting. Grayson, Moose, and Rona jumped in after him. Echo howled, and fled his rock bed.

Scraping his sore paws on sharp rocks, he managed to outrun them. He started walking across the unknown pathways leading to nothing but empty forests. He settled down on a patch of dead leaves that have fallen from the trees. He was about to turn back, like he always did.

But something held him back. Something strong.

Echo shivered. He swore he could hear wailing. He could also scent two wolves, one in his pack, and one that smelled like a pup, like fresh honey and maple trees.

He saw a shadow fly passed him like a bird. Echo frantically looked around, and then went running swiftly from the pile of leaves.

Echo followed the shadow, and when he reached it, Echo lunged at it with all his force. The big wolf howled loudly as the creature struck his shoulder. Echo quickly fled, running back to the trail. The shadow luckily didn't follow him. He slowed his pawsteps, now padding along the trail. He looked back where he saw the shadow; but it was gone. At least, he thought it was gone.

Two burning eyes, one green, one blue, shot to Echo. He panted, and started running again. The large wolf's heavy body was beginning to be stubborn and huge, slowing Echo down. He trudged along the trail, jogging.

His bushy tail was between his bulky legs, and his ears were against his head. Echo crumbled to the ground suddenly in defeat. He was lost, tired, hungry, and being watched by something unknown yet strong and swift. Echo closed his eyes. He was done for. These were his last breaths.

BOOM! Something struck Echo, and he quickly bounced up on his big, unsteady legs. Echo looks all over, but nothing was there. That's when he realised…

That shadow saved Echo's life. It awaked him from what he thought was death. It avenged him.

Echo thumped his paw on the ground. He was going to find a home… and a best friend.

Chapter 2

Echo and Willow trotted through the forest, side by side. Echo started glancing at the pup every ten seconds, just to make sure he was okay. He had never taken care of anything in his life. He needed to make sure this pup was okay at all times.

Willow started to notice. "You don't need to look at me so much," he laughed. "I'm not a newborn anymore!" Echo shook his head. "But you ARE a pup, and pups need care." Willows expression changed from amused to aggravated. "I've lived on my own for 6 months, I'm fine!"

Echo rolled his eyes. he guessed the small wolf wasn't as polite as he thought he was. "Okay, you don't have to yell," Echo said. "I was just trying to look out for you."

Willow looked away from Echo and murmured, "Sorry, I… I lost my temper a bit there."

Echo smiled. "That's okay," He started. "We all get mad. Now, let's hunt!" Willow's frown turned straight to little smile. "Let's get a deer," He demanded. "I love the taste of deer."

For the next 15 minutes, Willow and Echo searched the stream and the lush mossy ground. Finally, a deer was found. Willow lunged at it with full force, taking the deer off balance. It fell to the ground, and Willow scraped it's legs so it couldn't get up. Echo swiftly bit it's neck, and the life drained out of the deer's eyes. It was dead.

"Yum," Willow said, crouching down for a bite. "Wait! Lets play a game before we eat," Echo yelled. Willow rolled his eyes. "C'mon, I'm starving!" Echo smiled. "The game will get us even MORE food!"

Willow's eyes widened. "Tell me! What's the game?" Echo's icy blue-green eyes began looking sinister. "Let's see who can kill the most rats in 20 minutes. Willow smiled evilly. "Ready, set..." Echo wailed, "GO!"

The wolves ran off in different directions, Echo running towards the stream and Willow running away from it. Frantically searching the muddy ground around the narrow river, Echo found a rat. He dove at it, and bit it's neck. It quickly died. Echo smiled. "Yes," He said quietly to himself. "Echo one, Willow zero!"

For the next 15 minutes, Echo found no rats. He was beginning to become stressed. "Five minutes left, and you only have a single little rat? What an idiot, you are!" He whisper-shouted to himself. Finally, he found two rats huddled around a strawberry growing from the ground. Both of them were easy to kill. Suddenly, Echo heard a faint yell from a distance away. It was Willow's piercing voice. "TIMES UP, ECHO! Meet me at the deer's body!" Echo took the three rats' tails in his mouth, to leave them dangling, hitting his legs with every sprint. Echo wasn't ready.

Once he reached the body, it was devoured. Only small scraps of the deer's fur were left on the bones, along with the strong scent of wolf. Echo was furious when Willow came, he barely even noticed Willow had caught nine rats and a mouse to top it all off. "WILLOW, YOU SPIDER-NOSED HOG, YOU... YOU ATE THE DEER!"

Willow stepped back and dropped his rats and mouse. "What? I... I didn't do that, Echo! Smell me, and then smell that pile of bones. S-see? It's different!" Echo glared at Willow and then stepped forward to smell the bones again. He walked up to Willow and smelled him. They were different!

Echo glanced around for any wolves circling them. Suddenly, for a second, he saw two eyes glaring at him, a blue one and a green one. He gasped, and began shaking.

"Echo, scaredy-cat, stop staring at trees and stare at my rats and my mouse! I've got more than you! I win." Echo glanced up at him and shook his fur.

"Haha, y-yep, you won! Congrats, Willow... but, what will we eat now that the deer is stripped of its meat?" Willow gasped. "I can't believe it's wolfly possible to be that dumb..." Echo's face scrunched up in anger. "We've got twelve perfectly good rats and a mouse here! Let's eat them," Echo's faced softened, but he was still angry. "Okay, Okay, just shut up with the 'dumb' stuff. I'm not dumb!"

Willow laughed. "Okay, sorry," He said. "But I'm starving. Let's eat!"

The wolves lunged at the rats and easily devoured them. Echo ate eight and Willow ate four and the mouse.

After they finished, Echo said, "We need somewhere to sleep. It's almost sundown," Willow nodded, and Echo continued, "Nighttime is no place for a pup." Willow gritted his teeth and yelled, "I've survived 182.5 nights! I'll be FINE!" Echo nodded. "I know, I was just kidding. Do you have any ideas where to sleep.

Willow climbed onto a rock that jutted out of the ground. "Lucky for you, I'm the best shelter-searcher in the whole forest," He bragged. Echo agreed sarcastically, and followed Willow as he jumped down from the rock.

They scurried swiftly through the forest, avoiding rocks and thorns that had fallen out of roses. Finally, Willow stopped. Echo crumbled to the ground, whimpering. "My paws are sooooore! Nighttime is for sleeping, not running around the forest." Willow sniffed the air. "The shelter is nearby," He said, and continued running, Echo trudging after him.

The forest came to a stop, and a pile of rocks and flowers were in front of them. Echo lunged into them and snuggled up, asleep. "'Night, Willow."

Chapter 3

A warm breeze filled the air, along with the bright glow of the sun. Echo awoke, and took a deep breath. He could scent many things; Trees, grass, moss, two other wolves, and lots of flowers. He glanced over at Willow, who was bundled up in flowers and moss. Echo didn't want to wake him up, but he was starving. 'I'll hunt on my own,' he thought.

Turning back to the forest, Echo saw a shadow fly out behind a tree and lunge at him. It scratched him and scraped his face with it's dirty claws. Echo tried to run, but his cheek was gushing blood and he began feeling lightheaded. The shadow dropped onto him and bit his neck. Everything was getting dark. His vision was blurred and he couldn't feel any of his limbs. Suddenly, he couldn't see. He was blind.

Something shook him. Small paws patted his face, firm but careful. Echo opened his eyes. "I was trying to wake you. You were squirming around like a worm! I think you were having a nightmare. When I woke up, you were asleep, and had a huge scar on your face! It… It didn't look recent, It wasn't bleeding or fresh. But, you didn't have it yesterday, so…"

Willow continued talking, but Echo was too shocked about what happened. 'It had to be a dream,' He thought. But then he felt the scar on his

12

cheek. 'But… how could it be a dream when I have a scar?'

Echo tried to shake off the fact that he had a huge scar on his face, and turned to Willow. "So, should we start looking for some shelter?" Willow laughed. "THIS is our new home, Echo," Echo gasped. "No…" He said. "This isn't safe. It's out in the open where any predators could see us! Plus, this flower field looks too perfect. I bet the gorilla hogs made it, and when they come back, they'll see us and shoot us!"

Willow rolled his eyes. "Fine, fine, fine. I'd like to see what shelter YOU find. I bet it's gonna be a pile of deer poop!"

"Hmph," Echo said, and marched on into the forest.

It was a cold autumn day. Echo felt the frigid wind blow on his scar, irritating it. Echo gave the scar a quick scratch and then went onward. Once the wolves found a patch of moss, they sat in the squishy lush greenery and took a rest.

The stop didn't last for long. Echo needed to prove to Willow that he could find a good home, and he needed to quick. Echo trotted swiftly across the undergrowth, avoiding rocks and thorns. Willow didn't have much trouble keeping up with Echo; he was almost in front of him. Echo tried to speed up. He didn't want a pup to be faster than him…

As Echo ran, his paws became more sore, and his scar stung more. He wanted to stop, but he couldn't, for he needed to find shelter. Even though only the pup was relying on him, Echo felt a lot of pressure to find a great home.

Suddenly, a bright light flashed across Echo and Willow's eyes. Echo was startled by it, and jumped back. Willow stepped forward to sniff the air. "I think it was a sign that shelter is near," said Echo, a few steps behind him. "No," Willow said, turning his head towards Echo, "That was a gorilla hog's flashlight."

Echo tilted his huge head. "What's a flashlight?" He asked, embarrassed that a pup knew more than him.

"It's a ball of light woven into a piece of hard, grey stuff. It's called a flashlight 'cause it flashes and it's a light."

"Oh." Echo said, looking away from Willow. "I guess I was wrong. But, we can't be that far away from a good shelter." Willow nodded. "Maybe we can just find some moss and call it a day. We've been looking for hours!"

Echo frowned and shaked his head. "No, let's just look for fifteen more minutes."

The wolves trotted across the dirty undergrowth, stopping only when they heard sounds or smelled strange things. Suddenly, Echo stopped. His eyes glittered. "Willow…" He started. "Marshland!"

"Woah." Willow said. "I barely noticed the smell of wet grass!" Echo nodded. "And I barely noticed the forest starting to die down."

Echo stared in awe at the water and grass. "I've never seen one before. My mother told me tales of the marshland, and how she and my father had to cross it with their pack trying to find a good place to settle and build a town."

Willow looked up at him. "What were your mother and father like, Echo?"

"My mother was kind and helpful, and my father was brave and strong. Together they made the pack wonderful."

"If your parents were so wonderful, how did you get driven out of the pack?"

"I had a sister named Rona. She was really disrespectful to me, and my parents. One day, my father was teaching me how to catch a quick mouse, and we saw Rona barreling after another wolf. Me and my father thought she was just playing, but when we came back, Rona was there and my mother wasn't."

Willow's ears pointed up and his eyes glittered. He was listening to Echo with great interest.

"My father demanded Rona to tell him what happened to my mother. She said she had no idea. I thought she knew better then to not come clean to an ALPHA and her father, but I guess I was wrong. I never, ever saw my mother again."

"Once Barn was born, my life was a nightmare. He was such an idiot, and he did everything to annoy me and my father.

Every year, my father takes out all the pups for a hunting lesson. That year, it was just Barn and Grayson. Moose was going to come but he got sick when he ate a stink bug."

Willow snickered, but quickly flicked back to his serious listening face.

"Grayson went to practice alone, so father and Barn remained. Barn was practicing his crouch and he swung his back legs into my father's eyes. He was blinded, and he stumbled back. Barn found this the perfect time to practice his fighting.

He pounced on my dad… who was already weak from his years of being alpha, and his blind old eyes. He was easy to k-kill… it only took a few seconds."

Willow looked at his feet and nervously paced towards the water. He sat down and stared at it. "Sorry," Willow said, turning around and looking at Echo. His eyes were wet, like he was about to cry.

"But, Echo… if you weren't there, how do you know this?"

Echo's eyes widened a bit, as if he was surprised Willow asked that question. He wiped his face with his paw, licked his shoulder, and then sat down.

"U-um… my friend told me. Grayson… told me."

Chapter 4

"We were friends. Our friendship… sort of ended when he started being friendly towards Rona. But he still secretly liked me.

He knew he'd be executed if Rona found out her Delta was best friends with her dumb, lazy brother… so he kept it a secret. But when he chased me out, I… I guess I really assumed he would come back for me. But… he didn't. Why would you ever want a dumb oaf like me to be in your pack?!"

Echo yelled the last few words. Willow could see anger flashing in his eyes. '*Poor Echo…*' He thought.

"Don't say that!" Willow loudly said to Echo, but he wasn't screaming yet. "You are wonderful! You… you're like a father to me! But… more like a guardian angel descended from wolf heaven! You're great, Echo, really!"

Echo gritted his teeth, but then relaxed his tense shoulders and calmed his expression. He looked into the wet marshlands, and put a paw in the water. Then, quickly, Echo glanced at Willow and smiled. "Thanks."

Willow grinned, and pounced on Echo. They went tumbling into the water, and Echo hit a piece of wet grass. He turned around, ripped the grass off the patch, and threw it towards Willow. He laughed, and ducked under the water. "Careful," Echo said, and bit Willow's scruff, quickly pulling him above the water. Willow glanced at Echo.

He flew at him, and Echo fell under the water. Willow playfully bit Echo's tail, and he yelped. "Ow, stop, Willow!" He said, and kicked Willow in the leg with his paw.

Echo darted under the water, opening his jaw slightly. He coughed a bit, water flying through his mouth and into his throat. Suddenly, something flew into his fangs. He bit down on it, and swam to the surface. He jumped onto the grass, spitting the thing onto the ground. It was a fish!

Swiping his paw under the water, he picked up Willow and placed him on the grass.

"HEY!" Willow said, shaking his fur. "What do you want?"

"Fish! For eating!"

Willow stared down at the fish. "Woah!" He said. "I've never tried fish before. Can I have the first bite?"

Echo nodded and stepped back to give Willow a clear path to the fish. He pounced at it and almost devoured it. "Save some for me, Willow!"

Willow nodded and pounced back into the water. Echo rolled his eyes and quickly ate the fish. It was the most delicious thing he had ever tasted.

Glancing at the water and looking back at the spot the fish was in, Echo knelt down and licked the ground. He wiped his mouth and jumped back in.

Snoooort. Snort. Willows faint snores soothed Echo. He was laying on a pile of mushy grass. The swimming really seemed to tire him and Willow. He stared up at the starry sky, realising this is even better than sleeping in a small den or under a rock canopy.

Echo shifted his body to face Willow. He remembered what he'd said to him; Grayson being his friend.

Echo blinked and looked at his front paws. He rested his head on them.

Echo sighed. He missed Grayson… well, the old Grayson, at least. He was kind, even though he was slightly timid. He understood when Echo wanted to be alone, and when he did want to be alone, Grayson would always ask him if he was okay.

Echo closed his eyes, but quickly opened them. He wasn't ready to sleep! He wanted to try to come up with a plan to convince Grayson to live with him and Willow.

But How?

Echo would be instantly chased out if he even set paw on Rona's territory. He needed to find a way to sneak in.

Echo's eyes closed again. He had to admit, he was so tired he could sleep for a month. Echo decided to go back to sleep. He could go to his former neighborhood in the morning.

"Hey! Echo, it's morning!" Echo opened his eyes to see Willow's bright purple and yellow eyes, gleaming in the bright sunshine. It blinded Echo for a second. He wasn't used to sleeping in a place with no trees to block out the sun.

Quickly sitting up, Echo pawed at his mushy grass bed and quivered, with both nervousness and excitement. He had a plan to get Grayson; and he needed to explain it, and quick.

"Willow, we're going to my old town and getting Grayson to live with us. I'll tell you once we're in Rona's territory, and after I tell you, be very quiet. Grayson is brownish-grey and his eyes are very light blue. Like mine, but even lig-"

"WHAT?!" Willow interrupted. "I...I never agreed to this! W-what if I have an idea for what to do today?! Plus, this is COMPLETELY dangerous! Those wolves will rip us to shreds!"

Echo looked down at his paws. He had a feeling Willow would not agree. The rest of his life, Echo would never see his best friend ever again. He was disappointed. "I guess we can just hunt, then…"

Willow grumbled, and then sighed. "Fine," He said, with a sly smirk on his face. "But just 'cause I'm your friend! Oh, and 'cause I wanna see this 'Barn' guy, and… scratch his eyes out!"

Echo smiled. "Yes! Thank you, Thank you! Let's go!" Willow nodded and followed.

Echo was swift. He would get to see his friend!

Slowing down at some familiar mushy ground, Echo looked up. The narrow river was ahead of him and Willow, gushing and splashing aggressively.

Willow whimpered quietly. "D-do we have to cross it, Echo?"

Echo nervously looked at the stream. His eyes clouded with fear as he nodded slowly. "We… We do, Willow… Sorry…"

Willow closed his eyes and started to quiver a bit. All Echo could do was stare at his poor friend, waiting for him to be ready to get in. But he couldn't.

"Jump on my back. Hold on to my scruff."

Willow glanced up at Echo. Echo was afraid he'd be embarrassed or offended by his offer. But fortunately, Willow grinned a bit and nodded. "Okay. Thank you."

Echo jumped into the frigid water, a chill going down his spine. He was careful that Willow didn't get wet, thus Echo didn't shift his position or kick his tail very much so he wouldn't make any water fly up and spray Willow.

At the end of the stream, Echo jumped up onto the land. Willow padded onto the ground.

Echo glanced around, making sure no wolf was watching them. They were close to his former territory, and Echo didn't want to be harmed by his old neighbours, and he definitely didn't want Willow to be hurt.

Sniffing the air, Echo picked up a scent; the scent of over 20 wolves. All of them smelled relatively the same, all except for one. The wolf that smelled different had a peculiar scent, like the metallic scent of blood, along with honey, like the scent of a pup, but less sweet and friendly. Echo shivered, and inched his way into his old neighborhood.

Willow stepped on a branch, and it cracked loudly. Echo began to scent three familiar wolves, wolves he had smelled recently, along with a fourth wolf he didn't recognise but it still had the pack's scent. *HIDE!* He mouthed to Willow, and the pup barreled into a nearby bush.

Chapter 5

"What are YOU doing back here?" It was Barn, Moose, and a small female, cuddled up next to… Grayson.

Grayson let out a little gasp. "Oh my gosh, Echo, I am so sorry for chasing you out! I miss our friendship!" Grayson ran up to Echo, leaving the small female in the dust.

"Grayson, who is your friend here? Is she nice? I haven't seen her around. Is she a lone wolf?" Grayson's eyes sparkled at Echo. Echo smiled.

"This is my mate, Skyler. She was found alone in the forest. Her father betrayed her. Oh, and Sky, this is one of my old friends, Echo. He… he lives in the forest alone too." Grayson's face turned a bit red, and he shuffled his paws.

"YOU… YOU TRAITOR!" yelled Moose suddenly. "You still want to be friends with this idiot?! Fine with me! Get out of our territory or I'll make you!"

Grayson's ears flattened against his head, but they quickly perked up. "Okay, Moose! Bye! Say bye to Rona for me. C'mon, Sky!"

Sky trotted up to Grayson, with her head turned. She was really confused. Echo politely tilted his head to Skyler, and she smiled a bit. "Okay, I see what's going on. And… I'm glad! I've hated Rona."

"It's funny, really..." Echo said to Grayson as they trotted back to the marshland Echo and Willow slept the night before. "The exact reason I came to the town was to get you to live with me and Willow here."

Grayson nodded. "Well, good! I bet I wouldn't have had a chance to escape if you didn't come to... *save* me and Sky."

The rest of the day was uneventful. Willow and Skyler went to catch prey. Willow was surprised by Sky's hunting skills; She caught eight mice in just thirty minutes.

The moon began to rise, and all the wolves were asleep but Echo. He wasn't scared about something, he just couldn't sleep. He felt good, except one part of him was concerned.

Skyler's father. He had betrayed her! No wolf would ever betray their pup, especially if the wolf was as beautiful as Sky. Her eyes were sparkling light blue, like the color of the sky midday. Her fur was perfect, white and fluffy. She didn't have any marks or cuts, other than her ears. Both of Sky's ears were torn, which Echo thought was quite peculiar.

Suddenly, something patted Echo's back. "Echo? Echo, I need your help..."

It was Skyler's voice. Echo looked over at her. "What's the problem? Are you ok?"

Sky nodded, and nervously shuffled her paws on the mushy dirt ground. "I'm okay... I just smell something unfamiliar. It's not a wolf, I'm positive it's not a wolf. B-but... I'm scared, Echo!"

Echo sniffed the air. He smelled the slightly odd smell of the marshlands, along with Grayson, Willow, Sky, a strange smell of a wolf he didn't know, and the smell of something else.

"I don't know what it is..." He said, "But there's also another smell of wolf. Do you recognise that smell?"

Sky nodded, and her ears flattened against her head. "I think... I think I do..."

Echo gasped. "You do? I've been smelling it for days! Who is it? What is it?"

Sky opened her mouth, but quickly closed it and shake her head. "No, No, I... um, I actually don't recognise it. Sorry."

Echo disappointedly sighed, and sniffed the air again, trying to figure out what this unknown creature was.

Willow's ears perked up, and he jolted awake. "Why are you guys not asleep? The moon's still out!"

Before Echo or Sky could speak, Willow's nose began to tremble. He gasped quietly. "Dog."

"DOG?!" Sky yelled, her tail between her legs.

Willow looked at her calmly. "It's okay. Dogs are our descendants. And I don't even think it's a big dog. Don't worry, Skyler."

Suddenly, something flashed in front of the wolves. "What was th-that?" said Grayson groggily.

"It's a dog," Willow said to him. Grayson began panting nervously. "No, don't worry, it's small!" The dog seemed to be very quick, running in a big circle around the wolves. It seemed to be examining them, seeing if they were harmless or not. Finally, the dog skidded to a halt in front of the wolves. Sky stepped back against Grayson, who was trembling. Echo sat behind Willow, who seemed to be protecting him, although he was the youngest. "What do you want?" Willow asked the small dog.

"Oh, um, nothing. I just wanted to introduce myself, since you live here now. I'm Swift."

"What do you mean?" Echo asked from behind Willow. "Why would you introduce yourself? Do you live here? Why haven't we seen you around?"

Swift shook his small gray head. "I don't really live around here. I live across the marsh, in a house with my dumb old master. She's slow and wrinkly."

"What? A master?" Sky asked. "Are you talking about the gorilla hogs?"

The tiny dog laughed. "Ha, if that's what you call them. Anyway, I just wanted to say hi. Maybe I'll visit sometimes. Or even bring my friend Chestnut. She's long and brown, and she has long fur. I think

26

the masters call her a dachshund. And they call me a greyhound. I'm just two years old. I'll be larger soon…"

Swift blabbed on. Echo wasn't really listening. He was gazing out into the dense forest, scanning the trees for the burning eyes he had seen so many times.

All Echo could see was the forest. He could definitely smell something. Something like the smell he had scented all the times before.

I bet the wolf I've been seeing is Skyler's father, Echo silently said to himself. *I need to get her to talk to me! I need to know why this wolf is following me.*

"Well," Grayson said loudly, interrupting Swift's talking. "Nice to meet you, Swift. See you around."

"Bye!" Swift cheerfully yelped to him. "Have a nice night! Sorry for bothering you!"

"It's not even the night anymore," Willow mumbled, looking at the sun rising.

"Bye!" Sky said, and Echo nodded nicely at Swift. Willow shook his tail.

Swift bounded into the water, quickly swimming through it. He was a skinny dog, but Echo thought that was just because he had really short fur. "Maybe he can come over to eat with us," Echo said.

The wolves agreed. "That would be fun," Sky explained. "I like Swift. He has a lot to talk about."

"And maybe he can bring Chestnut over, too," Grayson said, licking his paw. "I'd be interested to see a *long* dog.

Echo blankly nodded his head, still staring off into the distance. He needed to get Skyler to talk.

"SKY," Echo suddenly yelled. "Let's go hunting. You're good at hunting. I want to see your skills."

"I'll come," Willow said politely. "I like watching Sky hunt."

"Maybe we can all come!" Grayson said, loudly. "I love big hunting parties!"

"No, that's okay, I wanna tell Sky something. You two can stay here."

Grayson winked at Echo. "Remember, Echo, she's my mate!"

Echo laughed a little bit, and bounded into the forest. "SKY," he said, when the others were finally out of sight. "Tell me about your father!"

Chapter 6

"My… dad?" Skyler whispered, her ears flattened against her head. "I… I'd rather not…"

"Just explain what he looks like. And what he smells like." Echo demanded.

"He… He's gray… with a white chest and paws. And snout."

Echo shook his head. "No," He said. "Tell me… his eye color."

"Amber and green."

"DANG IT!" Echo yelled. It echoed through the forest. *Dang it, dang it, dang it.*

"What's wr-wrong?" Sky said, her voice trembling and mumbly. "Are you alright?"

"No, I'm not alright. I mean… y-yes, I'm fine! I'm okay. Let's go back. I don't want to hunt."

"Wait, no," Skyler said, her tail blocking Echo's path back to the marshland. "My dad's eyes are green and *blue.* And his name is Shadow."

Echo stopped in his path. His eyes were wide and clouded. Echo was trembling immensely, he could barely keep balance. He felt the scar on his face. It was Sky's father. Sky's father who tackled him. Sky's father who saved him. Sky's father who scratched him. Sky's father that almost killed Willow. Echo couldn't figure out if he was bad or good. He decided Shadow was bad. He did one nice thing, and Echo thought he probably didn't even do it on purpose. He probably just thought he was attacking Echo again.

Suddenly, something jumped on Echo. It was heavy and had gray fur and bloodstained paws. It slashed Echo's ears, and he couldn't hear anything after that. It was all muffled. The big grey wolf's grunts, the sound of Sky screeching, "STOP! STOP!" Echo's own desperate yelps, all muffled.

"DAD! STOP!" Sky finally yelled, and barreled at the wolf. She caught the wolf off balance, and it stumbled to the ground. Sky whimpered and stepped back.

Echo could only hear her talking very faintly. "Dad, why have you been mafagick heakoh? Vuy haf tru…" Echo couldn't listen to anything after that. His ears were gushing blood.

Finally, a loud, deep voice was heard. The big wolf was speaking. "Oh, Sky," His voice boomed. "You are friends with this lump? He is ugly! He is fat! Do not associate with him ever! No, actually, I'll make it easier for you, Skyler, my daughter!"

Sky shook her head. "Don't, dad, don't, please…" Echo could barely hear what she was saying.

"I'll KILL HIM, HAHA!" Shadow yelled. "KILL HIM, KILL HIM, KILL HIM!"

This was it. Echo's last few breaths. He didn't know how he could get himself out of it. "I'll blind him first," The voice boomed. A big claw came down to Echo's face. He was going to be blind.

Suddenly, a wolf skidded in front of Echo, and the big claws came down onto his face. It was Grayson.

His dark amber eyes were scratched. Grayson was blind.

He licked his paw, and wiped his bloody scratched eyes.

Echo's eyes filled with tears. "Why... why did you do this? Don't be blind, Grayson! Don't!"

Grayson turned to Echo, his blind eyes shut. "Friends do anything for friends."

Sky ran towards Grayson and dug her face into his scruff. "NO, GRAYSON! NO! Don't be blind! Don't! Don't!"

Shadow smirked, and bounded away into the forest. His tail swooped into Echo's face as he ran away, his claws drenched with blood.

Echo sat next to Grayson. "Thank you, Grayson... thank you so much, thank you!" Grayson smiled and wiped his eyes again. "I'm definitely blind," He said, licking his paw. "But I still want to show off my *wonderful* eyes. I'm going to try to open them."

Right at that moment, Willow ran in through a bush. "What's up- WOAH! Are you guys okay?! Grayson- oh dung, you're blind, Grayson, you're blind!"

Willow patted Grayson eyes. "Ow," Grayson said, irritated. "Stop that."

"Sorry, I just want to make sure your eyes aren't still bleeding," Willow said, and wiped his eyes with a bit of moss that was nearby.

Once the bleeding stopped, Willow threw the piece of moss into the forest. "Who did this to him?!"

"My father," Sky grumbled, and claw the dusty ground angrily. "He's the biggest…pile of dung… ever!"

"Your father must be dangerous if he could blind a wolf this bad," Willow said. "We better watch out. Someone should keep guard every night. We could alternate."

"Sounds good," Echo said. "I'll do it tonight. I stay up late anyway."

"Okay, thanks Echo," Willow said. "Grayson, I think closing your eyes is making it worse. Can you open them?"

"Yes, I'd *love* to," Grayson said sarcastically, opening his scratched eyes. "How bad is it?"

"EEEEEW," Willow said. "It's all sticky and gross. Your eyes are all clouded. I assume you can't see, can you?"

"Nope," Grayson replied. "I mean, I can see a little. But you guys only look like blobs, and the trees look like green blobs, and the ground looks like a big brown blob with bits of green blobs."

"Yep, you can't see," Willow said, rolling his eyes. "But you can smell. You can smell us, and that would be an easier way to identify us."

* * * * * * * * *

This is boring, Echo thought. It was night, and Echo's first patrol. He sat in front of the sleeping wolves, sometimes padding around them in a circle.

It was the night of Grayson's injury. He was snuggled up against Skyler. Willow was on his back, snoring loudly.

All Echo wanted to do was sleep. He felt like he hadn't in years. *Why did I volunteer for night patrol?* he thought, sadly.

The night went by slowly. When the sun finally rose, Willow woke up and stretched. "How was night patrol, Echo?"

Echo was already asleep on the ground.

I might as well hunt, Willow thought, and walked into the forest.

Right away, Willow could scent tons of prey. Mice, rats, birds, squirrels... even some deer! He ran across the undergrowth, eager to catch some food for himself and his friends.

Willow stalked up to a robin, his mouth watering. He pounced onto the small bird, feathers spiraling into the air. Willow bit it's neck, and blood trickled down. "Perfect catch," He whispered, gobbling down the robin.

"Ah, Willow! Hello!"

Willow yelped loudly. "W-who said that? Get away! Rar!"

"Ha, Willow, it's just me, Swift. And Chestnut!" It was Swift. He looked like he had grown, although it had only been a day. His short fur was groomed, and it sparkled in the morning sunlight. The small gray dog was very handsome.

Next to Swift was a short, relatively plump female dog. She had long, wavy ears. Chestnut's eyes were dark brown, and her coat was the color of a squirrel. "H-hi there," The short brown dog said shyly.

Her voice was high and cute. "I'm Chestnut. I'm a dog."

"She's *pregnant,* whatever that means!" Swift announced, quite proudly. "I'm going to be an ol' father dog!"

Willow grumbled disappointedly. He had to admit; he had a small crush on Chestnut. She blushed, and hit Swift with her tail.

"It means I'm gonna have *pups,* you nut!" Chestnut yelled at Swift, pride and amusement sparkling it her eyes.

"Hey, Hey…" Swift replied to her, touching his nose to Chestnut's. "*You're* the one with nut in your name!"

Chestnut glared at Swift for a few seconds, and then pounced on him. Swift yelped, "HEY! Stop that, you- you-"

"-you nut?" Chestnut finished. "Exactly!" Swift replied to her, licking Chestnut's nose.

Chestnut and Swift laughed and licked each other for a bit. Willow felt awkward. "Uh, I'm gonna go get s'more prey now.... Um... bye." He trotted off.

"BYE WILLOW! SAY HI TO YOUR FRIENDS FOR ME!" echoed Swift after about a minute. "Bye," Willow yelled back to him. Quickly, he mumbled quietly to himself, "-and thanks for scaring off all the prey..."

Once he caught a few squirrels and dropped them back off at camp, Willow went on a walk by himself towards the river. Suddenly, an idea popped into his head. He could get Swift, Chestnut, and their pups to live with his friends, and they could have a... *pack.*

Chapter 7

"AHH! SKAPHEET! SKAAAAAPHEET!" The pup heard a human baby scream. She wished she could go deaf every time she went in her master's house.

She looked over next to her, at her sleeping brother. "MINT!" The pup whisper-shouted. "Wake up. I want to go outside, but mom says I'm not allowed to go without you!"

Mint rubbed his eyes. "Lola…" He said quietly. "Mom's at the… the vet… with master! She won't even know if you go outside, and the baby won't notice you."

"But what about Loren? She'll see me for sure!" Lola whined, shifting her paws nervously.

"She's upstairs. For goodness sake, Lola, calm down! Nobody will notice! Just go outside already!"

"O-okay. I'm trusting you! If someone sees me, I'll-" Mint quickly interrupted, "Yeah, yeah, you'll tell mom I put rocks under your pillow, and that I threw dead flies at you."

"Hmph." Lola grumbled, and walked outside, her head held high, but her tail still between her plump little legs.

The fresh smell of dew on leaves and freshly mowed grass flew into Lola's nostrils. She could almost hear mother nature telling her that her day would be good.

Lola padded to the fence and slipped under it. "I'm visiting Mochi," She announced loudly to Mint, who responded with a grumble.

Mochi was the plump french bulldog puppy that lived next to Lola and Mint. He had a sister named Pumpkinseed, but Mochi always said that 'she left to live in the tree place.' Lola never believed that. Who would pick a cold, dangerous forest over a comfy, safe home with great friends?

"MOOOCHI!" Lola yelled, scurrying under her friend's fence. "COME OUT!"

Suddenly, a plump little black-and-white dog stuck his head out the highest window in the house.

"Mochi? What are you doing up there?! Are you crazy?! You're going to hurt yourself!"

"Gee wiz, calm down, Lola! I bet I can safely jump from here to the fence."

Lola sighed. Her plump friend had always been a daredevil since the moment he was born. Mochi was only three months old and he already had jumped off four trees, jumped out of nine windows, and bit three babies.

Mochi's master put him in a cage whenever a child younger than six years old was in the house, but that meant Mochi was almost always in a cage, because his master had a five-year-old daughter.

Luckily, Mochi knew how to escape his cage, so his master finally decided to just lock him in the guest room with food and water for a few hours every day.

"Mochi, please get down! You're going to break all your paws, or even WORSE... break your NECK!"

"Shush, I can do it," Mochi replied to Lola, eying a nearby tree. "I'm going to jump from up here, spiral down, land on that branch, do... do a backflip, and then fall safely on my paws!"

Lola doubted that. But she couldn't do anything to stop Mochi from jumping...

Mochi looked like a bird with broken wings. Right when he was about to hit the ground, Lola dove where Mochi looked like he was going to land, and quickly sat down.

"WHAT ARE YOU DOING?! MOVE!" Mochi screamed, and then landed hard onto Lola. Luckily, Lola was a bit bigger than Mochi, and didn't hurt herself.

Mochi climbed off of Lola, panting heavily. "See? I'm fine!" Lola grumbled at him. "Now, what did you want to tell me?"

"Well, yesterday some people came to my house," Lola said, a little nervously. "I couldn't understand a lot of their words, but I heard them say 'away,' and 'adopt.' Are they going to take me away?!"

Mochi thought about it a bit, and said, "Yeah. They're probably going to take you away."

"NO!" Lola said. "I can't leave! I can't leave mom, I can't leave Mint, I can't leave you!"

Mochi looked at her sadly. "Well, if you are going to go, I want to say goodbye. You are a great friend, I will miss you."

" *LOOOOLA! COME BACK HERE, YOUNG LADY!*"

"Uh oh, it's mom, she's back! Ugh, I'm in big trouble… bye, Mochi… I'll really miss you. You were great!" Lola said, and ran under her friend's fence back to her house.

Surprisingly, Lola's mother didn't look angry. She looked sad, like she had just cried. Lola noticed there were some people she didn't recognise crowded around her and Mint's bed.

"You guys are going to be taken awa- I mean, adopted today. I… I won't see you again. I wanted to say goodbye. Goodbye, my beloved pups. I will miss you, a lot…"

"Wait," Mint interrupted. "You'll… you'll never see us… *ever* again?"

"…Yes, Mint. Sorry…"
Mint's eyes clouded with fear.

"I-is there a chance that *won't* happen?" He asked nervously.

"Only… if nobody wants you. But I doubt that will happen. I mean, you're just so cute and sweet, and… *OH!* I'm going to miss you guys so much!"

Lola's mother snuggled in with the small pups, her amber eyes glazed with tears. Lola could see she was upset and stressed. Lola really didn't want to leave her wonderful mother, Mint, and Mochi behind. They were everything to her. She would even miss her master, Loren, and the baby.

Just at that moment, Loren kneeled down to Mint, Lola, and their mother. "Pups…" She whispered in her raspy teenage voice. "I'll miss you guys. And I promise I'll keep your big mama safe."

She pet Lola's mother, and gave Mint and Lola kisses on their noses. "S-see ya."

Suddenly, a little girl swooped up Lola. "MOM! MINT!" Lola desperately yelled. "I DON'T WANNA GO! NOOO! I'M… NOT READY!"

"How much do you want for the-" The little girl's mother started to say, but the girl interrupted. "Can we name her?!"

Master laughed. "She has a name, but you can rename her. Oh, and, she's fifty bucks."

The women handed Master a crumpled piece of paper, muttering something Lola couldn't understand. The little girl looked at her. "I am gonna call you Chestnut! Hi, Chestnut!"

Chapter 8

"So, we can make a pack, just like Echo's old one, but… better!" Willow excitedly said to his friends. Grayson's clouded blind eyes looked interested, Sky looked eager, and Echo's jaw flopped open with awe.

"I think… I think Echo should be the Alpha. He has saved me many times, and he's really brave. He may not be the most agile, but he's big and strong."

"Yeah!" Grayson said, and Sky nodded happily. Echo smiled. He was happy, but nervous. He'd never ran a whole pack before. What would he do?

Skyler could tell Echo was nervous, so she kindly said, "Don't worry, Echo. You're only the boss of us three, and I don't even need to rely on you for everything. I can catch prey for me and Grayson."

"Th-thank you," He said to Sky, and then looked at everyone else. "Thank you all so much! I love you all!"

"Oh," Grayson quickly said. "I think Willow should be the Beta, even if he's not related to Echo, and if he's young. But from now on, I also think Echo should just be called Willow's father. I feel like they're really close, and Echo seems like a great dad."

Echo looked at Willow, waiting patiently for his answer.

"Yes." Willow finally agreed. "I'll call him dad now, even if it's not really the same. Except only on one condition; don't be overprotective."

"Of course I won't, Willow!" Echo said, frantically nodding. He wasn't like he used to be, glancing at Willow every second. A part of him relied on Willow, with his agility and smarts.

"Okay," Sky said. "Echo's Alpha, Willow's Beta… can I be Gamma?"

"Sure!" Echo said, and looked at Grayson. "So that means you're-"

"Delta," Grayson said, smiling. "I'm so excited about the whole pack thing. Except… I'm very sorry I'm blind. That means I won't be much help at all!"

"No, no, no!" Echo said, hitting Grayson playfully with his tail. "You are a big help, and it's all my fault you are blind. Plus, you can still identify wolves by smell, and you can see us, we're just huge blurs. You can identify us by our pelt color."

"Okay… thanks." Grayson responded. "Shall we hunt?"

"Oh, YES!" Willow yelled, relief flooding through his body. "I am starving. We can all go together!"

"Okay!" Sky said, happily nodding, but quickly glancing competitively at Willow.

Willow laughed. "I bet I can catch more prey than you!"

Sky shook her head. "Nu-uh, you can't. You're just a puny pup!"

Willow gritted his teeth. "I'm not even a pup anymore. I'm almost ten months old! Only two more months 'till I'm a big, bad wolf!"

Skyler's eyes glittered with amusement. "Okay, big bad wolf. How about… an hour. An hour of prey catching, then we meet at the marshes."

"Okay! Ready… set… GO!"

The wolves shot into the forest, their tails trailing behind. Echo smiled at them. Although he was afraid that Skyler's father might be out there still, he had a good feeling that they were going to be just fine.

Grayson's clouded eyes looked into the forest. Echo could tell he was nervous, but he couldn't blame the gray and brown wolf. The last time he went into the forest he was blinded.

"Don't worry," said Echo, glancing at him. "I'll help you go through. Or do you want to stay here…?"

"No, no," Grayson said, shaking his head. "You can take me in. But… just tell me when there's a rock or something. You can lead me around it."

"Yeah, Okay," Echo agreed, beginning to walk into the forest, Grayson at his side.

Echo began smelling prey. His mouth watered, and he was tempted to just catch a few mice.

Grayson seemed to notice, by the way Echo wasn't talking and his head looked like it was turned away.

"It's okay," Grayson said, amused. "I'll sit here. You go hunt!"

Echo hesitated. He didn't want to risk Grayson getting hurt again. "U-um… w-well…" He stuttered.

"No, really, go! It's fine, I'll be okay." Grayson protested. Echo nodded nervously, and trotted away.

So many smells! *There must be lots of prey lurking in the forest today…* He thought. Echo was glad there was so much prey. Thus, he easily found a target; a chipmunk, nibbling on an acorn.

Echo crouched, keeping his eye on the chipmunk. He lunged onto the small rodent, but before he could catch it a noise scared it off. "What? What was that?" Echo yelled, his voice quivering. "Who did that?"

He heard a deep laughing. Echo knew exactly who this was. He tried to run off. Echo needed to warn all his friends of the dangerous wolf!

"Where are you going?" The voice said, and something clamped on Echo's tail. "Stay a while."

"STOP!" yelled Echo, swinging his arm at the huge paw on his tail. He scratched the big paw with his claws, and it swung up in the air.

"Hey! How dare you hurt me?" The booming voice yelled. It was Shadow. "Ha," he said, his green and blue eyes glittering. Shadow examined

Echo, who seemed small to him. "And they call you an Alpha. You're just a fatso with no muscle."

"SHUT IT!" Echo yelled, scraping his claws against Shadow's face, making him stumble backwards. "Why did you betray Sky, you monster?!"

"Ah, finally, a tinge of common sense. That was a good question. And the answer is…" Shadow smiled ominously, showing his yellow sharp teeth. "I betrayed her because she was a horrible daughter. Her voice; Oh, goodness, that voice- It was earsplitting! I truly don't know how Grayson could like someone with such a terrible high voice. Oh, wait, *HE'S BLIND!*"

Shadow let out a screech of laughter, his tail waving. Echo's eyes squinted with anger and he bared his teeth. "I don't care if you kill me, Shadow. Just stay away my friends!"

Shadow's expression changed from amused to surprised. "Excuse me, Ech-poo, did you just talk back to me?"

"I did. Go ahead and fight me for it!" Echo snarled, his teeth still angrily clenched.

"Okay! Thanks, what a dear you are. Now, shall I kill you slowly and painfully or quickly and easily?"

Echo took a deep breath, quickly thinking about whether he should run and warn his friends or stay and fight. Before he could make a decision, Shadow lunged at him and bit the scruff on his neck.

"HEY! S-stop… that... ugh..." Everything went dark. Echo could feel blood trickling down his neck. Before he blacked out, Echo murmured, *Must… Save… Friends.*

The last thing Echo saw was Shadows broad smirking face, full of pride.

Chapter 9

"Echo? Echo, please don't be dead, please don't be dead!" Echo woke up, but he couldn't open his eyes, he couldn't speak, and everything he heard was muffled. He didn't recognise the voice that woke him, but it sounded quiet. It was a female, but not Skyler. Maybe not even a wolf.

Once Echo was finally able to open his eyes, he slowly looked at the creature looking down on him. At first, he didn't know who she was; but Echo could sort of recognise her. She was a dog. She had dark, big brown eyes, and a beautiful bronze pelt. Her body was long, with four stumpy little feet connected to it. Her words were muffled when she spoke.

"Oh, Echo, you're alive!" Her soft voice said. "It's me, Chestnut. Swift's mate… I was wondering if you wanted to see our pups, but obviously you can't, n-now that you're like this…" Echo tried to tell her he was okay, but when he tried to speak, nothing came out. He shrieked in fear that he would lose his voice forever. He could hear his scream. So could Chestnut.

"Echo, are you okay?" She nervously said. "Can you speak?" Echo sadly shook his head. Chestnut quickly let out a gasp. "I'm going to get your friends to come see you. Wait here."

Echo nodded and closed his eyes. He had a headache, his paws were sore, he couldn't speak, and his vision was blurred. A few minutes later, he heard the noise of tons of paws stamping against the ground. It was his pack.

"Echo?! Echo?!" Echo heard a young male say. It must be Willow. He looked at the small wolf. Willow's yellow and purple eyes were glazed with tears. "Echo, please, can you hear me?"

Echo tried to say yes. It came out like "Chyez."

"Yes? Does that mean yes?" Willow desperately said. "YEZ!" Echo said, louder. "Ih... staknd uap. Ih stake... Ih staned!"

"Do you mean 'I'll stand up?'" Sky asked, with Grayson leaning on her. Echo nodded. "No, no, Echo, I'll help you."

Sky bent down to help Echo up. His head started to feel a bit better as he walked to his mushy grass bed. As he was walking, Echo noticed that Swift was there. "Hi, Swkt," Echo said, looking at the skinny gray dog. "Hi, Echo..." He responded. "I... I know I haven't known you for long, but... I hope you're o-okay."

Echo nodded. "Ikm be kokuy. Ikm... be kokay." "Good." Swift said.

Echo trotted on. Soon, he got tired of Sky holding him up. Echo wanted to prove he was still a great leader.

"I... do it makself." Echo said to Sky. "Oh, you can talk better now. That's good. You can walk on your own, just be careful." Sky responded, kindly smiling.

Echo nodded, and trotted fast. Soon, he found himself away from his friends. He was in a place he recognised, but he couldn't remember where he was.

Echo's paws squished against the lush forest moss. He looked down at his paws. They were crusty with dry blood. Echo sat down for a rest to lick his wounds.

Licking wasn't helping. His cuts were stinging and still bloody. Echo decided to look for some flowers or moss to put on his cuts to make them hurt less.

Echo swiftly padded across the undergrowth, avoiding rocks and roots. He smelled lots of prey, but he was to determined to get flowers for his wounds before hunting.

Echo looked down, searching for any flowers. All he saw was dirt. He looked up at the forest in front of him, but there was no forest. It was a field full of flowers.

Echo's blue eyes widened as he stared at the beautiful landscape in front of him. He saw a pile of rocks and some moss. Suddenly, he realised. Echo was in his and Willow's old home.

"HEY!" A raspy voice yelled. Echo's ears perked up, and he turned around. A light brown dog with ratty unkempt fur that looked awfully like Chestnut was sitting in the field giving Echo the stink eye.

"What are yous doing on my territory?" He angrily said, growling. "Oh, um," Echo responded quickly. *Talk normally, talk normally, talk normally....*

"I... um, didnk.. Didn't... kn-know this was you'll... your f-field..."

The dogs eyes suddenly softened and his expression relaxed. "A loner, ey? Ah. I'm a loner too. You look like a *Husky*. What kinda dog are ya?"

Echo tensed. "I'm... not a dak.. Dog. I'm a wolg. Wolf." The little dog's eyes widened with fear. "Don't eat me, oh, please!" He said.

Echo shook his head. "I wonk-"

"Ha, just kiddin'!" The dog said, amused. "Are ya okay, wolf? You seem tah be talkin' weird."

"I'M NOT T-TALKING WEIRD," Echo said, surprisingly smoothly considering a minute ago he couldn't pronounce 'didn't'.

"O-kayyyy..." The dog responded. "Well, I'm a dachshund named Mint. I was never adopted. The humans said I was too *peculiar looking,* whatever that meant. Maybe it was 'cause of my lip!"

Echo glanced at Mint's mouth. His lip seemed connected to his nose. "It's called a cleft something-or-other. I forgot what it was called. Anyway, who are yous?"

"My name's… Eko. Echo." Echo stuttered. "I'm talking weird becoos… because… I just was fought, and my brain's all… werk… weird."

"Ah, okay." Mint said. "Do you gots a den or somethin'?"

Echo nodded. "It's near the marshland. Do you know where that is? My friends are prokably weiiry… worried."

Mint nodded. "Want me to help ya home? Or just point in the direction?" He asked. Echo quickly replied, "Okay, but… only half-way."

The wolf and the dog ran back into the forest. Echo felt better travelling with someone else. Whenever he felt dizzy, Mint would help Echo walk a bit.

The fresh, clean air also helped Echo. He could breathe again, something he couldn't manage to do when Shadow was fighting him.

Suddenly, Mint stopped and sniffed the air. Echo confusedly stopped too. "I smell something. Another dog, I think. Maybe even another dachshund!"

Echo sniffed the air too. It was Chestnut's scent. Echo heard the dachshund's high voice yelling "ECHO? ECHOOO?" faintly.

"That sounds like my old sister, a little bit," Mint said. "But it can't be. She lives with another owner very far from here. Anyway, I bet you can travel on yer own a little bit. Bye, Echo! See ya around, maybe. You're always welcome on mah field."

Echo said goodbye to Mint and then followed Chestnut's scent all the way up to where she was looking. Echo playfully hit her with his tail, and she spun around "ECHO!" She yelled, surprised. "Oh my goodness, are you okay?! All your friends are looking for you!"

"I'm okay, Chestnut, don't worry." Echo replied. "I think… I can talk fine again. My head doesn't really hurt an-anymore."

"Oh, good," Chestnut said, smiling. "Few. I'll go get your friends. Wanna come with me? You can tell me where you've been."

Echo nodded and followed Chestnut. They walked passed the spot where Echo fought Shadow, the spot where Grayson was blinded by Shadow, and the spot where Echo left Grayson to sit when he went to hunt. Echo's mind was full of horrible memories… but all of them seemed distant, like they happened years and years ago.

"It… was a long day. I'm pretty tired." Echo said, noticing the sun setting. "I wandered into this field of flowers, and met a dachshund that looked a lot like you. His name was Mint."

Chapter 10

Chestnut's eyes widened. They were full of fear, and excitement. "M-Mint?" She repeated, under her breath. "Mint!?"

"Echo, Oh my goodness, that's my brother's name! I left him when I was a pup! Did he have an owner, Echo!?"

Echo was a bit frazzled by her response. "He didn't. I think he was alone. Shall I take you to him?"

"No, no, just tell me which direction the field you found him in is." Chestnut said. Echo pointed his tail behind them. "That way."

"Okay, well. Um, now let's find your pack." She said quickly. "Thanks…"

The animals swifty galloped through the forest, calling their friends' names. Finally, once they reached the Marshlands, they got a response.

"CHESTNUT?" It was Swift's voice. "Chestnut, have you found him-" He ran in front of Echo and Chestnut, panting.

"Ah! You're okay, good, good… I'll get the others, and then maybe you can come see our pups. How does that sound?"

Echo nodded. "That sounds good."

The wolf and the dogs trotted back into the forest, and Swift called out loudly. Sky and Willow ran up to them, greeting Echo and talking about how glad they were that he was okay.

"Hey-- where's Grayson? Is he alright?" Sky nodded. "We didn't really want to make him have to walk around for long, with his eyes and stuff. He's taking care of Chestnut and Swift's pups. It seemed to be okay that he was blind, he just needed to make sure he could smell them. Plus, they were asleep when we showed them to him."

"How did your guys' owners allow an untamed wolf into your house?!" Echo asked, surprised. Chestnut shuffled her paws on the ground and Swift shifted his position a bit.

"W-well," Swift finally said after five seconds of awkwardness. "I left my owners to live in the wild with Chestnut and the kids."

Willow nodded, and Sky embarrassedly licked her chest. Echo's jaw hung down. "You lived in the wild this whole time?!" Echo yelled loudly to Chestnut.

"I'M SORRY I DIDN'T TELL YOU!" She yelled, her tail drooping down. "I didn't know how you'd take it… if you'd be glad, or angry that I'm in your forest. I moved here ever since Swift told me about you."

"It's FINE! It's actually great… and it makes the question I was going to ask you even easier for you to agree to!" Echo happily said.

"What's the question?" Chestnut responded.

"Would you, Swift and Chestnut, agree to join our pack? Along with your pups, who could grow up in it?"

Swift immediately yelled, "YESSSS! YES!" Chestnut didn't say anything, but the huge smile on her face said it all.

"I'll get Grayson!" Sky said, and excitedly ran to get her mate. The animals rejoiced.

Once Skyler came back with Grayson and the puppies, Echo happily told them the good news. The pups were awake, and they seemed excited, too, even though they didn't understand what was going on.

"Okay, okay," Echo announced loudly. "If we're going to have a pack with… um… *nine* animals in it, then it's gonna have to be structured. First of all, Chestnut, your pups need names!"

Chestnut smiled. It was obvious she had already chosen the names; just by the look on her face.

"Well," Swift said happily. "Me and Chestnut chose some names for two of our three pups, but the other one, we're not very sure what to name her."

"This…" Chestnut said, pointing her nose to the biggest male pup, who was a light brown (lighter than Chestnut) dachshund. "Is Tango." The pup's stumpy tail wagged and he let out a little yelp of happiness.

"And this is Stream." Chestnut said as a pup emerged from behind her leg. It was a little gray and white long-haired dog that had the fur of Chestnut but the shape of Swift.

"Finally, this little guy's name is undecided." Chestnut looked at the smallest pup. She was all gray with blue eyes.

"Hey!" Willow said, glancing at the pup and then looking back at Echo. "She looks a lot like you, Echo! With those crystal-y blue eyes and gray fur."

"GREAT!" Swift yelped, his ears perked up. "Her name will be Crystal! Yes! Thank you for the suggestion, Willow!"

Willow's eyes widened with surprise. "Well, you're welcome, I guess, but that wasn't a sug-" Echo hit Willow in the back with his tail and awkwardly smiled at Swift. "Yes, you're welcome!"

"Anyway, we need proper bedding and dens if we're going to have a pack. So, let's start building our new town!" Echo yelled. The animals agreed, and got to work.

"Hey," Skyler said. "How 'bout we make one huge awesome cave that we can all sleep in, and you get your own den because you're Alpha!"

Echo blinked. "G-good idea! Um, w-well, I'll start building my den, I guess, and all you guys can work on yours! Heh!"

Echo trudged to a blank spot in the forest. He hesitated, turning around to look at his friends, laughing and building. *Together.*

The next couple of days went by quickly. The camp was beginningcoming to look really good. Working next to his friends taught him much more about their personalities, likes, dislikes, and even hidden talents. Echo never knew Sky loved building so much, and that Swift didn't like how fish tasted. He even learned new things about Grayson, someone Echo knew his whole life.

Finally, the dens were finished. They were spacious and comfortable, with room to spare even when all the animals were in it.

Day after day, the friends talked, hunted, and mentored Chestnut's pups. Before Echo knew it, the pups could speak.

"GOTCHA, STREAM!" Tango yelped as he bit Stream's leg. "Oww, Tango, Ugh! I've told you so many times I didn't like playing *let's get Stream!*"

Tango groaned. "Seriously, Stream? You're no fun at all! Live a little!"

Stream rolled her eyes and padded away, stumbling a bit. None of the pups got very used to walking yet, since they slept so much.

"Siblings," Echo said, sitting next to Swift watching the pups play. Swift nodded. "You gotta love them, though."

Echo hesitated. He didn't love his sister… was that wrong of him?

Finally, Echo nodded rapidly. "Yeah, hah, you gotta love them for sure." Swift agreed. "Do you have any siblings, Echo? I do. Lots and lots of them."

"TELL ME ABOUT YOUR SIBLINGS," Echo said loudly, ignoring Swift's question. "O-Okay then," Swift said, surprised by his yelling.

"Well, I never really see them anymore," He started. "They all enter these crazy running and jumping races. They've been doing them since they were two years old. My mother never let me enter them, since I was the smallest and youngest. That upset me a bit, but I knew she was doing it for my own good.

I have seven siblings. Rain, who is probably… fourteen now. He was the oldest. Then there's Snowy, she's probably ten now. Oh, and Moon, who is probably eight now. His twin is Moss, and she's eight too… and then River, who is seven now, I'd say. Also, there's Mango and Berry, twins again, who are… five or six, probably. Oh, and finally, I'm three. Anyway, do you have any siblings, Echo?"

Echo looked at his paws."Um… No. None."

Chapter 11

Echo sighed. It had been a week since he had lied to Swift, and he still felt guilty.

Echo had decided to go on a walk with Willow, since the small wolf could always find a way to make Echo feel good.

But… Willow seemed to keep quiet. He did exactly what Echo was doing, padding slowly, occasionally crouching to catch some prey.

Echo turned to Willow. "Are you okay?" He shrugged. "I dunno. I feel a bit sick, but I think I'm going to be okay. A little stomach ache can't kill me..."

Echo stopped. "Well, i-f you need to stop, that's okay. Or do you just want to go home?" Willow glared hard at Echo. *Did I do something wrong?* Echo thought, nervous.

"You think I can't take it? You think I'm weak?" Willow said, annoyed.

"N-NO! Not at all, that's not what I'm thinking at all!"

"FINE! I'LL JUST GO!" Willow yelled, running into the distance. Echo sat down. *How could I have made Willow angry so quickly? He's usually the happiest wolf I know. He must be really sick.*

Suddenly, Echo heard a thud in the distance. "WILLOW!" He yelled, running to where he heard the noise. "Are you oka-"

Willow was lying in the middle of a patch of dirt, quivering. "Echo..." He whispered, his voice shaking. "I... I really don't feel good. Take me home, p-please..."

"Okay! H-hang in there, buddy, you'll be okay!" Echo said, swooping up Willow onto his back. He could feel Willow's raggedy cold fur against his own. Willow was really sick.

"WOAH! Is Willow dead?!" Sky yelled once Echo and Willow got to the dens. "No, he's just really, really sick! Help!"

"Oh! Let me help with him!" Grayson said, sniffing the air to follow the trail to where Echo and Willow were. "When I was in the pack, whenever a wolf was sick Rona would... *order* me to see to them. I can identify what sickness it is, but I'm not so good at finding any herbs that can help."

Echo remembered when Grayson used to take care of him when he was sick. He thought about the time he had a fever when he was about two years old. Grayson told him to stay calm and rest a lot. That helped.

"Yes, yes, just please do anything! Thank you!" Echo cried. Grayson carefully sniffed Willow. Echo very softly placed him onto his bed in the den.

"Pneumonia," Grayson finally said. "He just needs to rest. Or eat. I think he might be malnourished a bit."

"W-will I die?" Willow whispered, his voice quivering. Grayson smiled and shook his head. "No, you won't die, you just need some rest. Oh, and talking will do you no good. Shush! Go to sleep."

Willow blankly nodded, before instantly falling asleep. Grayson trotted back to where he was sitting with Sky, and Chestnut and Swift continued watching the pups tumble around. Only Crystal seemed to be shocked by Willows sudden sickness. Her eyes were clouded with fear.

Echo spent the night with Willow. He couldn't sleep. *I hope Willow is okay...* he thought. *I hope what Grayson said was true. I can't have Willow die on me. I can't deal with that.*

Echo rested his head down onto the soft grass. He could hear faint snoring of his friends, and occasionally one of them whimpering in their dreams. Echo wanted to stay in the big den more than his own. It was somehow more calming and peaceful.

Although Echo didn't want to leave Willow, a strange force seemed to be pulling him towards the water in the marshes. *Maybe...* Echo thought. *The water just might wash all my worries away.*

Echo rose up, being careful not to disturb Willow. The moon was full tonight, shining on the water, almost giving it a glow. Echo quietly padded over to the water.

He had always been interested in water and sea animals ever since he had been just a pup. Echo's father taught him everything a wolf could ever need to know about water. How to tell if it's not good to swim in, how to tell if it will be full of fish. Echo sat in awe as his father explained everything about water, from water in the huge ocean to water in a puddle.

Echo's father's name was Stump. He was a big brown and gray wolf with dark brown eyes. His mate was Lilac, a sleek agile light gray wolf with the most beautiful blue eyes Echo had ever seen. Crystal reminded him of Lilac a lot, with the same fur and even the same eyes.

Echo placed his paw into the glittering water. It was warm and made Echo's whole body tingle. He carefully inched his way into the pond, drenching his pelt with hot water.

Finally, Echo was in. He didn't know what to do. Swimming was only fun with others. *Stupid,* Echo scolded himself. *How'd you come up with an idea like that?!*

Echo slipped out of the water, heading back towards the den with his friends. Abruptly, he stopped. If he slept with them he would get water everywhere…

Echo trudged back to his private den. It was actually the first night he slept in it. All the other times he was either building it or sleeping with his friends.

Echo sat down on his grass bed, almost expecting a tumbleweed to fly past him. He was lonely.

Echo shook his wet fur, splattering the rock and mud walls of his den. He could hear the wind whooshing around outside, making Echo shiver.

Suddenly, Echo heard a loud whimper. His head spun around. It was one of Chestnut's pups! It was... Stream!

Echo sprang out of his bed and lunged to the pup. She was deep in the water, yowling and paddling. The little drowning pup looked exactly like Willow when he was drowning a year ago. But to Echo, it seemed like that happened just yesterday.

"...STREAM!" Echo yelled, galloping towards the water. He plunged in, the coldness of it giving Echo a shiver down his spine.

"E-Echo? Echo, h-h-help!" Stream screamed in despair. Echo nodded frantically, quickly rushing up to the pup, holding her hard by the scruff. Echo swam fast, heading for the shore. Suddenly, he lost grip on the small pup, and she went plummeting into the water.

Echo yowled, plunging under the water. He needed to save this pup. He knew he could. *If I saved Willow a year ago, it means I could save this pup now. I could probably save her faster then I did with Willow, too, since I've grown stronger over the months!*

Echo's confidence replenished his body again. He shot towards the screaming pup, aiming for her scruff again. He fastened his teeth down, biting down on her neck.

The pup seemed to calm down a bit, but she was still yowling.

Echo was still underwater. He felt he was running out of air; well, both him and the struggling pup. Echo felt his own life being sucked out of him. Was he about to risk his life for a scrawny pup?

He jumped out of the water onto the shore. Echo was alive, but Stream was nowhere in sight. He turned around to see her lifeless body on the grass.

Chapter 12

"OH MY GOSH, WHERE IS STREAM?!" Chestnut screamed, waking everyone in the pack up. "Stream… is… g-gone!"

Swift gasped "Our pup is gone?!" He immediately looked at Echo, seeking help from the pack leader. "What do we do?!"

Echo hesitated. Should he tell them? He knew he had to. He sighed.

"Last night," Echo started, tears glazing his deep blue eyes. "I saw Stream in the marshes. She was drowning, I thought…" Chestnut leaned on Swift like she was about to faint. Echo continued sadly. "So I jumped in, b-but I couldn't save her. I… I'm really sorry. I'm not cut out to be the Alpha. I… need to go."

Echo turned around, running into the forest. He could smell plenty of different things; wolves, stray dogs and cats, prey, even some gorilla hogs. But, Echo wasn't paying attention to that. Bad thoughts flooded his mind. *I'm not going back. I can't go back. But… I need to! They need me! Or do they? Am I a bad leader? Am I a bad wolf? Should I have killed myself from the start? When I just got kicked out? I wish I did. I wish I was dead right now.*

Echo stopped and looked up at the rising sun. The sky wasn't blue yet, it was a mixture of pink and blue. "I'm really sorry…" Echo whispered, his eyes sparkling. "I'm really sorry, Stream…"

Suddenly, two wolves pounced onto Echo, toppling him over. Echo yowled. "STOP! BACK OFF!" He gave the two wolves warning scratches and they growled and backed off. They looked familiar. *OH GOSH,* Echo thought, his fur beginning to stand on end. *It's Shadow! And... and... who's that?*

Shadow's eyes widened. "Ah, Ech-poo, you're back. How are you? And how's your little blind friend, hmm? Well, actually, that doesn't matter, 'cause you won't see him ever again, will you? Hmm? You want to die?"

Echo growled. The female wolf next to Shadow gagged. "ECHO?" She yelled, her sinister blue eyes sparkling with surprise. Suddenly, Echo recognised the eyes. It was Rona, his sister.

"RONA!?" Echo screamed, trembling. "What are you... how are you... how do you know Shadow? What about the pack? Did they finally kic-"

"Mama?" Echo heard a small voice say. A little gray wolf with green eyes walked out from behind Rona. He seemed young... very young. Echo assumed he was only a few months old.

Rona's head spun around, but Shadow kept glaring at Echo. "Bloodmoon, it's not a good time," Rona snapped at the pup. His little ears flattened against his head.

"Wh-who's that, mama? Is that your daddy?" The pup squeaked. Rona shook her head quickly.

"Bloodmoon, please, just… scram for a second!"
Shadow said, annoyed, flapping his paw at the pup.
He turned around and walked away, his tail
drooping. Echo could hear Bloodmoon mumbling,
"Hmph… you never tell me *anything*… about your
past, your family, your old pack…"

Rona turned back to Echo. "Echo, get out of here,
or I'll… I'll… kill you!"

Echo sat down. He wrapped his tail around his
paws, just like he used to sit when he was on his bed
in Rona's town.

"Now, Rona and Shadow," He started. "I do not
want to fight. I just need to tell you guys
something."

"BE QUICK OR WE'LL KILL YOU FASTER!"
Shadow screeched, shaking with anger. Rona hit
him with her tail. "Stop it, you lunatic," She
snapped at Shadow. Rona looked back at Echo.
"Talk already, creep!"

"Well," Echo said again. "Rona, in the past you've
done… um… bad things. And Shadow, you… you
have too." He swallowed. "I think that you guys
should just stop overreacting and… start minding
your own business. Just leave me and my pack
alone, please. Please."

Shadow lunged at Echo, scraping his claws against
his neck. Echo fell on the ground, gurgling blood.
"DID YOU REALLY THINK YOU COULD TELL
US OFF WITHOUT GETTING A…

PUNISHMENT?!" Rona screeched, joining Shadow. Echo yowled with pain.

Suddenly, Bloodmoon ran out from behind a tree, lunging at Shadow. He bit his tail, and Shadow screamed, turning around. Bloodmoon quickly scratched Rona's eyes, and started yelling in a cute pup voice, "RUN, WOLF, RUN!"

Echo ran as fast as he could for as long as he could. He couldn't think. He couldn't talk. He could barely even breath. *A pup...* he thought. *Younger than a year old... just saved my life. I am pathetic. I am no leader.*

Echo slowed down when he started to recognise the world around him. He stopped to hunt a bit, and soon caught a fawn. Echo gulped it down easily; he hadn't eaten in days.

Suddenly, Echo heard a happy bark behind him. It was Swift's. "Echo! There you are," He said. He let out a sad laugh. "The pack has searched for you so much times over the past few days."

Echo nodded. "I'm so sorry…" He said, looking down at his dull-clawed paws. "I killed Stream. I couldn't save her. If only… I was a good leader. A noble Alpha. A boss you could rely on. Sigh…"

Swift shook his head. "NO, NO, ECHO! We love you! All of us! You are amazing, really. Stream's… Stream's death was an accident. I know it. I mean, you didn't WANT to kill her!"

Echo shrugged.. "Swift…" He mumbled, looking

up at the white and gray dog. "From now on, I will be the best leader ever. I will be great! I will take care of everyone. And I will actually sleep through the night. Hehe."

Swift smiled. "Yes, you will, big guy!" He yelped happily. "And you will do it with me, Chestnut, Grayson, Sky, and… Willow!"

Echo agreed. "Could we go back now? Back to the pack?" Swift nodded and grinned. "Yes we can!"

The wolf and the dog walked back to the dens, side by side. The grass felt soft on Echo's paws. He felt like he could be ready for anything, even a sudden attack.

"Echo is back!" Sky announced once Echo walked to the big den. She was organizing some prey on the ground. Grayson was next to Willow, who seemed to be feeling better. Chestnut turned around. Her two remaining pups were snuggled against her. She looked upset.

"Oh, hey," Chestnut said, wrapping her long body around her pups and settling on the ground. Tango glared at Echo, but Crystal didn't. She had a faraway look in her pretty blue eyes.

"Echo," Crystal finally said in a small, nervous voice. "What happens when you die? Where do you go? Where did Stream go? Can… can I still see her?"

Echo looked down at the little gray pup, almost identical to him. He shrugged. "I'm sorry, Crystal, I don't know."

"WOLF! GRAY WOLF! HEY!" A voice suddenly yelled. Echo spun around. It was Bloodmoon, the little pup that saved his life. He shot towards him.

"Blood... Bloodmoon, is it?" Echo said, smiling. "Yes! And you are...?" Bloodmoon chirped happily. "Echo. I'm Echo." Echo announced. "Pleased to meet you!" Bloodmoon squeaked in reply.

"Thank you, Bloodmoon, thank you so much!" Echo yelled, to everyone in the pack's surprise. *Why is he welcoming a total stranger?* They thought, staring at the green-eyed pup. Bloodmoon didn't seem to notice at all.

"Oh, everyone," Echo said quickly, turning over to his friends. "This is Bloodmoon the pup. He saved my life when Rona and Shadow almost killed me! He's-" "Who's RONA?" a chorus of Echo's friend's voices said. Echo told them the whole story, with Bloodmoon blushing next to him.

Chapter 13

"So," Willow asked Echo that night when everyone was asleep. He was almost recovered, but he still didn't feel the best yet.

"Bloodmoon's living with us? He's in our pack?" Echo started to shrug, but stopped himself and hesitated. "Uh." Finally, he nodded. "Yeah. He's living with us. I mean," Echo's eyes glinted with amusement. "He saved my whole entire life!"

"And so did I, Grayson, Chestnut…" Willow started, being quickly cut off by Echo "Well, yeah, and they're all in the pack. How did you and Chestnut save my life anyway?"

"If you didn't find me, then you would probably have been eaten by a bear or taken away by a gorilla hog or something." Willow said proudly. *Oof,* Echo thought. *He's right…*

"How did Chestnut save my life?" Echo asked, ignoring what Willow had just said. "She's the one that found you in the forest. If she didn't, then you would just be wandering around- and again, be eaten by bears!" Willow laughed. "Shut up," Echo snapped.

"And if you're going by the logic that finding me in the forest is saving my life…" Echo said, smirking evilly at Willow. "Than Swift has saved my life too."

Willow rolled his eyes. He had never really liked or respected Swift. Willow always thought Swift was snobby; even though he wasn't. He also didn't like that he was Chestnut's mate. *He* wanted to be Chestnut's mate.

"Go to sleep, Willow," Echo demanded to the gray wolf. "Fine." He grumbled, laying his head down. Echo trotted out of the big den back to his own.

Echo curled up on the grass, easily falling asleep. It had been a tiring week.

In a snap, Echo was awake again. *Wow...* he thought, looking at the walls of the rocky den around him. *It was a fast night.*

Suddenly, the walls started to fade away, and Echo found himself in an empty field. It was windy, and the sky was gray and cloudy. Fog was everywhere.

Something was calling Echo's name. It sounded like it was very far away. Echo squinted his eyes and looked around. It was hard to see with the immense fog.

ECHO. ECHO. ECHO. His name seemed to be repeating over and over in a pattern. "Yes? Yes? What do you want?" Echo nervously yelled. "What can I do? What can I do?"

A hoarse voice called out his name again "Echo..." It started to say. Echo frantically nodded. "We need you! All of us!"Many different voices all yowled with agreement. Echo still couldn't see any of them.

"What do you need me for? Who are you?" Echo called out, looking into the sky. Suddenly, all the clouds moved away to make a gray sky appear. Hundreds of stars twinkled above Echo.

"We need you to… go to the…" The loudest voice said again. "Across the marsh… to the town… and get… get…"

"GET WHAT?" Echo screamed desperately. "The wolf! the… the white wolf! The stray! The… scarlet eyes!" The voice called out. "I will bring her a message too! Get her, Echo! You're the only one!" The voice faded away.

Echo could hear the words echoing in his mind over and over. *You're the only one…*

"Good morning, Echo!" A small voice said, waking him up. It was Bloodmoon. He was sitting with Crystal, eating some rats. "Yeah, morning!" Crystal said, glancing at Echo and then back at her food.

Echo rose up and stretched. As he padded out of his den, Echo began feeling pressured. Should he really cross the marshland to find some random wolf? Was he going to risk his life because of a silly dream?

Echo sighed. He remembered when he was a pup he would have nightmares, and would frequently wake up squealing. Echo's father's words always calmed him down. "Dreams are there to tell you something. Some dreams, usually nightmares, might tell you to toughen up, or even that you are doing something wrong. Echo, you are stronger today then you were yesterday. I can see it in your eyes."

Echo smiled as he started remembering his whole entire childhood, splashing in streams and playing with his friends and family. Nostalgic thoughts flooded his mind.

"Guys," Echo finally said to the two pups. "Tell the pack I will be back in a few days. Willow is in charge. If he is still sick, Grayson is in charge." The pups nodded, and went on talking.

Echo padded up to the marshes. He could feel his heart start to beat faster, and his fur tingled. It was an unpleasant feeling.

Echo splashed into the water. Crystal's head turned. "What're you doing?" She asked, Bloodmoon staring at him behind her.

"I just need to... um... tell someone something. They live... across the marshland... with the gorilla hogs." Echo mumbled, just loud enough for the pups to hear. Bloodmoon continued to talk to Crystal, who kept watching Echo struggling to cross the marshes.

"Ew," Echo said once his friends were out of sight. "This is gross..." The dirty, smelly water clung to his fur.

"This is my home, y'know!" a voice suddenly snapped. It was a white wolf with golden eyes, padding out from behind a tree on the edge of the marshland.

"S-Sorry! I was… just…" Echo yelped. "Ha, that's okay," The wolf laughed. Her voice was raspy, but she didn't look too old. The white wolf was the same age as Echo. "I was just kidding. What're you doing out here? You seem like a woods wolf." She asked.

"I… was, um… just taking a look!" Echo said, his voice quivering. Was he supposed to tell, or keep it a secret? "No you weren't," The wolf replied. Echo opened his mouth to argue, but she quickly interrupted him. "But that doesn't matter. I'm Sunflower, but I prefer being called Sunny. Sunflower is too girly."

"I'm Echo," Echo said to her, waving his bushy gray tail. He sighed. "Actually, you're right… I didn't come here for a look. Something in a dream told me to cross the marshes, and… find a white wolf… with scarlet eyes…" Echo suddenly realised how ridiculous he sounded. "It's stupid, really…"

"IT IS NOT!" Sunny yelled. "Weird wolves come to me in dreams all the time, and lemme tell you, they're not there for no reason!" Echo shrugged. "Then what does it mean?"

"Well," Sunny said. "I know a wolf like that."

Chapter 14

"WHO?!" Echo shouted, jumping out of the dirty water onto the grass. "Poppy, my younger sister," Sunny said. "She lives farther down the way you were heading. Once you reach the part of the marshland with all the big rocks in the water. Me and Poppy used to climb all over them, pretending we were those hiking gorilla hogs…"

"Thanks!" Echo yelled. He was already down in the water.

An hour later, Echo finally reached the rocks Sunny was talking about. He turned, climbing out of the water. "POPPYYYY!" Echo yelled.

"Hhm?" He heard someone say. They seemed far away. "Who goes there?" The high voice said. A white wolf emerged from behind one of the big rocks on the grass. "Who are you?" She said.

"Echo, I've met Sunny." Echo replied, jumping out of the water. "Oh, hi. I'm--" "Poppy?" He asked. The wolf nodded. "Why do you need me? Does Sunny need something?"

Echo shook his head. "In a dream… someone told me to cross the marshland to find a white wolf with scarlet eyes." Poppy's red eyes glinted. "Well, that's me… but why did someone want you to meet me?"

"I don't know…" Echo said, looking down at his paws. "I knew it was silly…" "It's not!" Poppy yelled. "Dreams have a meaning, and I think I know the meaning to that one. Y'see, I think I've been being followed by someone, but I've been... um... too afraid to try and catch that creature that has been watching me. I think It's a wolf... I've only seen it's eyes. Green... and blue, I think."

"I KNOW WHO THAT IS!" Echo yowled, walking past her to look into the forest. He saw nothing, except for trees and grass.

"BEHI-" Poppy suddenly yelled, but it was too late. Something was on top of Echo, attacking him.

"AUGH!" Echo grunted, pushing his body up to make the wolf on top of him fly off his back. The wolf yelped as it flew into a big, sharp rock.

"Shadow! I knew it!" Echo snapped, glaring at the dark gray wolf. He could feel Poppy's trembling fur brushing up next to him.

"Smart," Shadow said, blood trickling down the gash in his shoulder from the big sharp stone. "I know what you've been doing, Echo. You and... that *DISGRACE* of a pup have been living with each other! I cannot believe my own son betrayed me and Rona, my wonderful mate. I was teaching him to be the nastiest wolf in the forest! I guess he did seem a bit distracted during our training."

"Save it, Shadow!" Echo shouted. "Bloodmoon is a great, intelligent pup! He is one of the best wolves I know! I am not going to let you just yap on about how horrible he is, because he's NOT. I'm not going to let you yap on about any of my friends. You are going to be killed!"

Echo lunged at Shadow's throat, biting down hard. He yowled in pain, swiping his paw across the huge cut. Blood gushed out everywhere. Shadow tried to yell, but all that came out was blood gurgling in his throat.

Echo barreled onto him again, scratching and biting until Shadow went limp onto the ground. Echo touched his tail against his empty body. Shadow's heart wasn't beating. He wasn't breathing. He wasn't moving.

"ECHO!" Poppy yelled, touching her nose to his pelt. "You saved me! Oh, how can I repay you?! I love you so much!"

Echo smiled. Perhaps they could be mates. Or was it too early? *No, no,* Echo thought. *It's early, but... I don't care. I think I do love this wolf back.*

"I'll take you to my home, Poppy. Do you want to... live with me and my pack?" Echo asked.

"You have a whole entire pack?!" Poppy squealed. "Echo, you're too much!"

Echo laughed. "Come, I insist!" The white wolf nodded. "Wait," Poppy said. "Lets sleep here. It's too late to swim. Plus, It would take forever and the water is freezing!" Echo agreed, and let Poppy lead him to her den.

"Home sweet home," Poppy said joyfully as she patted down on her wet leaf bed. "I'll go get some leaves for you, too, Echo."

Poppy's walked out of the den, her tail waving behind her.

Suddenly, Echo regret his decision. Did he just mate with a random wolf he happened to save? He barely even knew Poppy. What was she like around other wolves? Is she friendly? Does she like dogs?

Once Poppy returned, the wolves shared a bit of prey she caught while getting the leaves and went to bed.

Blinding sunlight woke Echo up. He didn't have any dreams that night. The strange voice must've been happy with him.

After he woke up Poppy, the wolves left. Echo wasn't really in the mood for swimming for so long again, so he and Poppy walked along the edge of the stream until the grass started getting marshy and the trees disappeared.

"Gross…" Poppy said, looking at the murky water and soggy grass. "Ha, yeah, it's pretty nasty. But you gotta do what you gotta do." Echo snickered.

He splashed in, but Poppy hesitated, looking squeamishly at the water. "Er… no thanks…." she mumbled.

"The water's great! Please come in, Poppy!" Echo said loudly. Poppy closed her eyes and jumped in.

Her eyes quickly opened with surprise. "It's cold, but... doable."

Echo laughed and waded onward. Suddenly, a familiar raspy voice yelled, "Ey! Over here!" It was Sunflower.

"Sunny!" Poppy shouted, her ears perked and her tail waving happily. Poppy started moving towards her, but Sunny shook her head. "I'll come to you!"

With a big splash, Sunny came barreling into the water. "Hey, guys! Where ya going?" She asked.

Poppy looked down at the water. "Well..." She murmured sadly. "Echo's taking me to live with him and his friends. I'm glad about that, because I'm usually pretty lonely, but I don't think I'll see you again, Sunny..."

"Ah, sis, I'll visit you!" Sunny yelled, lunging playfully into her sister. "It's just forward from here, right, Echo?" She asked, glancing at Echo. He nodded.

"Okay! Now Poppy, go, go with Echo! See you soon!" Sunny said, pushing Poppy away. "Bye!"

"Now," Echo said to Poppy when they were just a minute away from the dens. "My friends will welcome you, not hurt you. They are friendly. Don't be afraid."

Poppy nodded, and swam swiftly to the shore, her head held high. She was excited... Echo could tell.

Chapter 15

"Echo, you're back!" Chestnut yelped happily when he and Poppy arrived. "And... who's this?" Echo smiled. "A new member in our pack! This is Poppy, my... my..." He mumbled the last words. "M-mate."

"Mate?!" Willow yelled, running to him, a mad, confused expression on his face. His purple and yellow eyes glinted with anger. "Echo! You have a mate? But... but... now I'm the only one without a mate!"

Echo nervously smiled. "Willow! Heh... you must be feeling better. How are you?" Willow growled. "Don't change the subject, Echo!" He snapped.

Echo blinked. "Look, you'll find a mate sometime! You're a great little wolf!" He said in protest. Willow shuffled his paws. "I don't need a mate. They're gross, anyway. With all their curling their tails around each other and licking each other... Blech! I'm going to hunt." Willow marched off.

Echo felt Poppy's soft fur fluffing up against his own. "I thought you said your friends were nice, Echo." Echo nodded and stared into the forest. "They are, Poppy. Don't... worry."

Poppy shrugged. "Can I see our den?" Echo nodded. *Poppy could sleep with me.* He thought. *I mean, she is my mate. She... is my mate.*

"You're gonna sleep here with me," He said,

staring at his small grass bed. Echo would have to make another one. *At least I won't be lonely now.* He thought, glancing back at Poppy's brilliant scarlet eyes.

"Cool," She said, looking around. "Can you introduce me to everyone?"

That's exactly what Echo did. He noticed Poppy seemed to love the pups; maybe she wanted to have pups of her own. Echo liked the silly little puppies. Maybe having some real pups of his own would be nice.

"The puppies are really cute. I've always wanted pups." Poppy said to Echo as they walked back to their den. She settled down on the cold dirt ground.

"I'll get you a bed after this," Echo quickly added before Poppy started talking again.

"Thanks." She said. Echo thought Poppy would say something else about the pups, but she didn't.

Echo's eyes met Poppy's. She blinked kindly. "Thank you for bringing me here. I appreciate it." Echo dipped his head to her. "No problem."

Echo couldn't fall asleep that night. He felt he was stressing over nothing; Willow was okay, the journey to get Poppy was short, Bloodmoon and Poppy were both welcomed nicely... but Echo still was worried. Had he made the right decision picking a mate so quickly? He only had known Poppy for a few minutes until he had fallen in love with her.

Poppy was beautiful. Her wonderful scarlet eyes, her soft white fur. Echo felt her pelt rubbing against his own. Poppy's quiet breaths were synchronized with his own. Suddenly, Echo felt nothing was wrong. He had a full pack. He had a mate. He had friends. Shadow was gone. Rona probably left the forest or went back to her own pack when Shadow died. Echo was safe.

Or… was he?

Echo woke to soft pawsteps outside his den. "Good morning, Tango, Crystal, and Bloodmoon." He said as the three pups went bouncing past him.

Crystal turned around. Tango did after her. Bloodmoon did too. "Why did you kill Stream, Echo?" Crystal said. "Yeah, Echo? Why did you murder our sister?" Tango said, with the exact same lifeless tone as Crystal. Finally, Bloodmoon spoke. "Will you kill us, too?"

Tango and Crystal repeated after him. "Will you kill us too? Will you kill us too? Will you kill us too?"

Echo woke up in a cold sweat. He stepped outside. It was still dark out, and there was a freezing breeze. Echo's gray fur fluffed up in the cold.

He sat down and looked at the moon. It was full, and looked almost blue-ish. Echo blinked. The words bounced around his mind.

Will you kill us too, Echo?

Will you kill us too?

Echo felt really, really guilty. Had he really killed a pup? He looked down at his paws. His claws were outstretched, like he was ready for battle. *I am a murderer.* He thought sadly. *I am a horrible, terrible murderer.*

'Echo...' Echo suddenly heard someone say. The voice was a sweet, high pup voice. He immediately knew who it was. 'I forgive you. It wasn't your fault, after all. Stop focusing on me... and start focusing on someone else.'

Stream's voice faded away. *What does she mean?* Echo thought nervously. *Who should I pay attention to? Bloodmoon? Poppy? Willow? It has to be Willow, right?*

"HEY! STOP THAT!" Echo heard a voice yelling. He must've fallen asleep outside. Echo rose up, embarrassedly licking his paw.

"I'll only stop if you let ME start out with the prey!" Tango yelled, his stumpy paws on Bloodmoon's belly. He grumbled loudly. "Stop that! Fine, you can have the prey first! Now GET OFF!"

Echo heard Swift snicker. He looked over at the dog. Swift's yellow eyes glimmered with amusement. "It's like they really are brothers," Echo whispered to him, smiling.

Tango's ears perked up, and he turned to Echo and waddled up to him. "Oh, good morning Echo! Uh… want some prey?" He said, his raspy little voice almost shaking. It was obvious he wanted to impress Echo.

Tango ran up and snatched the rat out of Bloodmoon's mouth. "Hey!" Bloodmoon yelled. Tango ignored him, and trotted back to Echo and dropped the food at his paws. "It's… pretty fresh. Sky caught it like an hour ago."

Echo looked down at the prey. It was covered in dirt and grass, and Echo felt he could even spot some deer poop on it. The pups must've been rolling it everywhere.

"Thanks for the offer, Tango, but… that's okay. You guys keep playing!" Echo said, smiling. "Yeah!" Bloodmoon said, bouncing up and snatching the prey from Tango's paws. Tango opened his mouth to protest, but then just drooped his tail and grunted angrily.

Just then, Crystal walked out of the forest. *Was she alone?* Echo thought, looking at the little gray pup walk along to the den. She seemed to be carrying something in her mouth.

"What's that you got there, Crystal?" Echo asked, stopping Crystal. She looked at him and dropped itin on the ground. It was blue and long, with a silver oval hanging off it on a small silver ring. "I think it's a collar," She said, looking down at it.

Echo didn't recall ever hearing the word collar. Suddenly, he remembered his mother telling him about it; *collars* were something pets wore so their gorilla hogs would know who they were.

Echo crouched down and examined the collar. He looked down at the silver oval. It said in block letters, **BREEZY.**

"Breezy," Echo said. Crystal repeated it back. "Breezy… who's Breezy?" Echo shrugged. "Must be just a dog that wandered into the forest and left their… collar here." He said.

"Yeah, probably…" Crystal admitted, sounding kind of discouraged. Echo assumed she was looking for adventure.

"Probably just a dog." Crystal said again. "Just a dog."

Chapter 16

It had been a week since Crystal had found the collar. She had been keeping it tucked under her grass bed. Crystal was determined to figure out who 'Breezy' was. She didn't believe Echo. It had to be important.

"Be right back," Crystal yapped to Chestnut that morning. She ran into the forest, right back to the spot that the collar was. Crystal waited. *The dog must come back to get their collar. It's the most important thing to them, other than their master.* She thought.

Suddenly, Crystal saw a shape fly past her. She frantically looked around.

This has to be the dog! Crystal thought eagerly. *Oh, what if they want to join the pack? I must tell them! Echo will be so proud!*

"Greetings, Breezy!" Crystal yelped happily. A brownish-gray dog with only one dark brown eye skidded up to her. His paws were gray and cracked and his eyes were wrinkled and droopy. To Crystal, he looked as old as ever.

"What is a stupid furball like YOU doing in MY meeting spot?! And m'name's not BREEZY, It's FREEZE! My old idiot master named me that pathetic name! It's horrid!" His voice rasped.

"Hello, Freeze." Crystal said, confidently. She wasn't afraid of the big dog. "I am Crystal, a fellow dog. I found your collar."

"Collar?" Freeze rasped. "Dog?! I'm a wolf! A cheese brain captured me and sold me to a crazy idiot master! He did that with all my family! Finally, a few days ago, my wolf instincts took over and I bit my stupid master and he kicked me out! But I don't care, the forest is better than his itchy blankets! I don't mind! I don't CARE! Who needs a collar?! I put it here so I could never see it again! I live here, It's MY meeting spot! MY forest! MINE, MINE, MINE!"

Crystal blinked. It was obvious the old sack of bones was mad; She could see it in his single eye.

"I don't mean to upset you," Crystal politely said. "But... I'm afraid this isn't your forest. It's Echo's forest."

Freeze's eye widened. "Who is this idiot, ECHO? If he's the owner of this forest, then why haven't I seen him around? I swear, If a dumb furball like you is lyin' to me, I'll rip your stupid tail off!"

Crystal sat down. She was starting to grow impatient. "I'm sorry, Freeze, it really is Echo's! If you would like to meet him, I would be glad to bring him here," she said softly.

"Great! I can rip *his* tail off too!" Freeze yelped, along with a strange screech that Crystal assumed was a laugh.

"Well, if you are going to do that, then I will not bring him to you," Crystal said, a bit annoyed.

Freeze howled. "BRING HIM TO ME OR I WILL MAKE YOU CHANGE YOUR MIND!"

"Fine." Crystal mumbled, turning around. "Stay here."

"Echo?" Crystal said once she came back to the dens and went into Echo's. "Are you awake?" Echo rose up and tiredly smacked his lips. "Now I am. What's the problem?"

Crystal told him everything; about how she didn't believe him, how she went to the forest, how she met Freeze. Echo seemed quite astonished.

"And... you're taking me to this psychopath?" Echo finally asked after Crystal finished talking. "Um, yeah," she said, with a nod.

"Okayyyy," Echo said, nervously following the little gray pup into the forest. "Let's see who this is."

"Freeze?" Crystal asked once she saw a glimpse of his unkempt ragged pelt. "EH?" Freeze shouted, turning around. A shiver went up Echo's spine when he saw Freeze's ugly face and single eye. The other eye was closed, with scrapes scratched across it. Dried blood was all over that eye.

"Ah, this is Echo!" Freeze yapped in his raspy old voice. "Hello there, 'leader of the forest'! You are a big old idiot! I'M the leader of the forest, don't you know, stupid hog!? Get out of MY forest or I'll rip your stupid fur off!"

Echo tensed. "I… am not the leader of the forest, Freeze. I just live here. Crystal just made a mistake. No need to… rip my fur off."

Freeze blinked. "A mistake?" He repeated. "Ha! I figured from a stupid pup like that one!" Freeze swiped his tail across Crystal's body, knocking her over.

"Woah, woah, no need to be rude, Freeze." Echo said, helping Crystal up. "We aren't here to confront you. I actually would like to leave you alone, but we live quite close to here so if you stay then you probably will be disturbed by us. I'm sorry, we just usually hunt here."

"Me? Disturbed by you and your dumb furball cousins?! No, no, no! YOU get out of here! My territory! Grahr!" Freeze snapped.

Echo sighed. "We can't move. I'm really sorry. This is my home, and my pack's home."

"Oh-ho-ho! And now you have a *pack?!*" Freeze yelled. "Lies! Lies, I tell ya! You idiots just want me to leave! But I won't!"

Crystal looked up at Echo. He seemed as impatient as she was. "Okay, well, I'm just gonna leave with Crystal- but please don't come and bother our pack. We won't bother you." Echo said with a groan.

"Maybe I will, maybe I won't. Now scram!" Freeze shouted at them.

"He's mad." Crystal said to Echo as they padded back to the dens. Echo nodded. "Hopefully he doesn't bother us."

Once Echo and Crystal returned, only Chestnut, Grayson, Willow, and the two pups were awake. Swift, Poppy, and Skyler were still asleep.

Bloodmoon ran up to Crystal and greeted her, before pulling her away to play with him and Tango. Willow was talking to Grayson, and Chestnut was eating her breakfast.

Echo's stomach rumbled. He walked over to a bit of deer on the ground and brought it over to Chestnut. "Good morning, Echo," she said to him, taking a bite of her prey. "Morning," Echo replied, setting down his prey.

Chestnut looked up at the pups playing together. "I'm glad they all get along," she said. Just then, Tango pounced on Bloodmoon and he yelped in anger. "Well, sometimes," she said with a laugh.

Echo nodded. Suddenly, confidence rushed through his body. He was the Alpha of a whole entire pack. He had a mate. He had friends. He had food. This was what it was like to be a respected leader.

And Echo loved being respected.

Chapter 17

"Wow!" Willow said. He and Echo were gathered around a strange bug. Echo reached out his paw and carefully dabbed the bug's hard shell. It rolled up in a strange oval.

Echo and Willow were hunting. They had found a bit of prey, but not a lot. Willow got distracted by seeing the bug, and asked Echo to see it.

"What do you think it is?" Echo asked. Willow shrugged. "I don't really know, but it's definitely not a beetle or any bug I've ever seen."

"Hey-- maybe we can ask Swift! Once he told me he was an expert with bugs because his sister, Moss, always told him about them!" Echo yelped happily. "Good idea! I'll go get him; stay here and make sure the bug doesn't leave."

"'Kay," Echo said, his eyes fixed on the peculiar bug. The past few weeks had been tiring, and Echo was glad everything was- or, almost was- back to normal. It had been about two months.

There was no sign of Freeze, so Echo had thought he probably left. Everything was calm now. Echo could relax.

A few minutes later, Willow came back with Swift. "Where's the bug?" He asked, looking around. "Here," Echo said, pointing his nose to the little gray oval.

"Oh, that's easy! A roly poly, obviously." Swift said, looking at the weird insect.

"Hah, that's a weird name!" Willow said, looking at the little roly poly.

Swift smiled, a bit evilly. "They're also really tasty," He murmured darkly, and swooped down to eat the bug. "BLECH!" Willow and Echo yelled at the same time.

This is great, Echo thought. *I feel like a pup again... getting into mischief with my friends. I barely even feel like an Alpha.*

"ECHO! ECHO! Poppy is... Poppy is..." Chestnut suddenly yelled, running on her stumpy legs to the boys. She sat down and started to pant.

"What?! What is it?!" Echo shouted, the fur on his belt bristening. "She is PREGNANT!"

Excitement and fear shivered through Echo's spine as he followed Chestnut back to the camp, struggling to keep up. His legs felt so weak and trembly.

"Echo!" Poppy chirped, blinking happily. "Isn't this great? We have pups of our own!" Echo nodded. "Yes... great!" He said, his tail waving happily. Poppy's pink belly stuck out. It was obvious she was pregnant. How could Echo not notice it before?

Echo felt cold. He started shivering a bit. Bad thoughts popped into Echo's mind. *What if it turns out just like Stream? What if... I accidently kill another pup?*

Poppy looked at Echo, confused. "Uh, Echo? So...?" she asked, her ear perked up curiously. "Huh? What?" Echo finally said, snapping out of his terrible thoughts.

"I said, what should we name them?" Poppy asked, blinking. "Well, It depends on what they look like, right?" Echo replied, staring into her scarlet red eyes. Poppy hesitated, but then nodded slowly. "Yeah, Okay."

The next day, Echo took the pups out to train a bit. He remembered how his father always did that; taking the youngest wolves out for a hunting session. Echo felt a bit pressured to follow his father's footsteps, but another part of him felt happy and proud to do it.

"Echo," Bloodmoon said curiously, eying the water. Echo and the pups were next to the river where he saved Willow from drowning. "Can you teach us how to catch fish?"

Nostalgic memories flooded Echo's mind. He remembered how he saw his father teaching the other pups to catch fish... and then being killed. Echo tried to shake that thought out of his mind.

"Sure!" Echo finally replied, leading Bloodmoon and the others to the water.

As he taught the pups to fish, Echo kept thinking about the same thing: all his friends. Especially his dead friends, like his parents and Stream. Echo would never see them again… never hear their voices, never see their faces… ever again.

"Echo?" A rough voice interrupted. It was Tango. "Are you there?" he said, amused. Echo nodded. "Y… Yeah. Let's get back to fishing."

The next day was uneventful. There was no need for hunting, because the day before they got so much food it could last a couple of weeks.

Nobody really had anything to do. The pups played with Swift watching them nearby, Chestnut and Poppy sat in front of the marshland talking, and Willow was teaching Grayson how to hunt blindly. Echo sat on a patch of moss watching them all.

Suddenly, Crystal rose up and ran to Echo. "Be right back," She said, padding swiftly into the forest like she was late for something. "Okay…" Echo replied, but Crystal was already in the woods.

Chapter 18

"Freeze?" Crystal whispered as she stepped into the forest. "Are you here today?"

Suddenly, she saw a quick shadow fly past her. Crystal knew immediately it was Freeze.

"Whaddya ya want, kid?" A raspy voice called back to her, and Freeze skidded to a halt in front of Crystal. She blinked. "Well... in our pack there are more pups coming. And... I really want to teach them like Echo taught me, but I think I'm too young. I mean, I'm still pretty much a pup."

The old wolf nodded. "You are a still a pup, indeed," he said to Crystal. "But maybe if you manage to learn as much as you can before the pups are born, that stupid Alpha could stop eating grubs and realise you're pretty smart."

"Echo's not stupid..." Crystal muttered. "And... how am I s'posed to learn so much in such a quick amount of time?"

Freeze smiled at her. His teeth were cracked and blackened. "That's where *I* come in!" He announced. "Every day, you come here, and I shall teach you all that I know!"

Crystal shrugged. "But..." She said. "What if the pack notices and gets suspicious?"

Freeze blinked. He hadn't thought of that. "Well..." He rasped. "Just tell 'em you're hunting! And... actually hunt on yer way back!"

Crystal's eyes glinted. Even after visiting Freeze every day for almost two months, she still couldn't decide if he was a good guy or a bad guy. He was nice to Crystal, but... would he be to anyone else? Freeze did always insult Echo and the rest of the pack.

"I guess." She finally responded. "But... I don't really want to lie to Echo. He's a great wolf-"

"YOU'RE NOT LYING!" Freeze pointed out. Crystal immediately shushed him. "The pack will hear!" She whisper-shouted. Freeze rolled his eyes.

"You'll figure it out." He said. "But for now... goodbye." Freeze called as he stalked into the depths of the forest.

Crystal sighed, and walked back to the dens. She knew at some point she'd need to tell someone about her meetings with Freeze.

"Ah, you're back, Crystal!" Tango yapped when Crystal returned. "Where were you? Why are you always gone in the mornings?"

Crystal didn't respond. She flung her tail up to Tango's mouth and led him behind Echo and Poppy's den where no one could see them. She raised her tail up so Tango could talk.

"WHAT'S THE BIG IDE-" Tango shouted before Crystal shushed him again. Tango's ears flattened against his head. "What is it?" He grumbled.

"The thing is..." Crystal whispered. "Every day I've been visiting this one wolf...." Tango gasped, and Crystal swung her tail over his mouth again.

Tango scratched it, and Crystal yelped and waved it down.

"His name is Freeze. He's old, and wise. And tough. You'd like him. But who he is doesn't matter. Well... y'see... you know how Poppy is having pups?" Tango nodded, his ears curiously perked up. "I sort of want to teach them... like Echo teached us. Even though *I'M* still a pup. It... It sounds stupid now..." Crystal trailed off, shaking her head.

"It's not *that* stupid..." Tango said, grinning kindly (Something he rarely does). "I'm pretty interested in training a pup too. Even though.... I'm still a pup."

Crystal smiled. "Well... I'm glad you understand. Promise you won't tell?" Tango swore he wouldn't, and then walked off to join Bloodmoon again.

Crystal let her shoulders relax. She really didn't think her rude brother would be so... considerate. Crystal padded off to the main den, settling down, ready for a hard-earned rest. She had barely slept the night before.

"Ahh!" Echo moaned happily as he walked out of his den, stretching his legs. "Morning!" Echo chirped to the pups, and they nodded back to him. Echo had a feeling it would be a great day.

"Hey, Sky and Grayson," He said to the two wolves. "Hello, Echo," Grayson said, his ears perked up so he could hear everyone's voice. Skyler smiled at Echo.

Poppy and Chestnut were sitting sharing a fawn. They had developed a great friendship, mostly because they were the only females that weren't really wrapped up in anything else, unlike Sky, who needed to care for Grayson, or Crystal, because she was always playing or exploring with the other pups.

Echo waved his tail happily, greeting them. "Hi!" Poppy and Chestnut said at the same time, and then laughed at each other.

Echo looked around for Swift, but he wasn't there. Only Willow, who seemed to be staring off into space, lost in his thoughts. Echo walked up to him.

"Hey," He said. Willow blinked and quickly turned his head towards Echo, like he was startled by him. "Oh, Hi!" Willow responded. "What's up?"

"Do you know where Swift is?" Echo asked. Willow shrugged. "Probably hunting," He said. Echo nodded in agreement. "Do… you want to hunt with me? I mean, if you're not doing something…"

Willow shook his head. "Oh, no, we can hunt!" He said, and sprang up. Echo smiled and said, "Okay, let's go!" And they were off into the forest.

The wolves spent almost all day hunting. Echo loved every minute of hunting with Willow. He was great at making Echo laugh. They got a total of twelve rats and three mice. Fifteen delicious pieces of prey.

During the hunting break, Willow asked Echo, "What will you name your pups?" Echo shrugged. "Well…" He said. "I really want one of them to be named Marigold. Hopefully there is a female." Willow agreed. "Marigold is a nice name."

Echo smiled. "Hopefully they will hurry up!" He said. Willow smiled. "Just, like, two more months, I bet!"

The next month went by pretty quickly. The pack did what they always did; hunt, train, fake-fight. The puppies were growing up quickly, and Poppy's new pups were on the way.

Everyday, Crystal still visited Freeze. Freeze did train her very well, and he did make her a much better fighter and hunter, but Crystal started getting worried about him. Freeze was becoming very old and run down. After the month ended, Freeze could barely win a fight against Crystal. Crystal was certain he was going to die soon…

Chapter 19

"Okay," Freeze rasped one day. It was the third of March. All the snow was melted away by the blazing sun. The flowers started blooming, and the hibernating animals woke up from their long winter rests.

"In only a few weeks, the pups will come, and my time will be up," Freeze announced. Crystal tensed. *What does he mean by... 'my time will be up?'*

"I will not be needed by you anymore." Freeze said. "You, Crystal, are the only one I am staying alive for. Nobody else visits me. Nobody else even really *knows* me like you do, except for my idiotic old owners." He spat on the grassy ground angrily, remembering his horrible past. "I will have to die once the pups come. I only have very little tips left to tell you, very little stuff to teach you. So, on the first of April, I will die."

Tears formed in Crystal's eyes, but she quickly blinked them away. "No... no... don't die!" She shouted. "How do you even know you're going to?! You... you might not!"

Freeze shook his head. "A strange voice in a dream told me," He said, looking kindly at the pup. "I know... it's stupid to believe a random voice in a dream... but I do. I know I will die."

Crystal sat down. "Fine... but, if you are going to die, *please...* can I make these days leading up to your death... amazing ones?"

Freeze smiled, but his eyes looked sad and faded. "Very well," He said, dipping his head down. "But starting tomorrow. I'm very tired. You must go back to the dens."

Crystal nodded, and trudged away, her tail drooped down. She wanted to save Freeze from death… but… how?

"Hello," Poppy said once Crystal returned. She and Grayson were the only ones there. Sky wasn't even with Grayson.

"What's going on?" Crystal asked, looking around. Poppy's expression darkened. "The others saw three intruders, all of them were black and white wolves with red eyes…" She mumbled, looking down at her paws. "They didn't know who they were, but… they looked really creepy, so they went after them."

Crystal looked over at Grayson. He was asleep, but he wasn't in one of the dens. "Is Grayson okay?" Crystal asked. Poppy nodded. "He was tired, but he said he smelled a stink bug in his bed, so he slept here instead."

Suddenly, the whole rest of the pack returned. Luckily, everyone looked okay, just a few scratches. Well, they did at first glance. Crystal realised Skyler was leaning on Echo with a huge gash on her shoulder.

Grayson must've smelled her blood, because he sprang up from his nap and ran over to Sky, licking her giant cut with his warm pink tongue.

"Is everyone else okay?" Grayson asked, looking around. "Yes," Everyone said. "The pups, too?" He said again. "Yep…" Tango said. "Yeah! Chestnut, Chestnut, tell Grayson what I did!" Bloodmoon squeaked.

Chestnut nodded to him. "Bloodmoon scratched one of the wolves' eyes and blinded him for a long time so he was easy to kill," She said to Grayson. He smiled. "Good job!" He said to the pup. "Thank you!" Bloodmoon said proudly, and ran off to tell Crystal, who was standing nearby.

"Will Skyler be okay? I don't want her to die!" Echo frantically asked Grayson. He nodded. "I can't see her gash, but I think it'll be okay. I don't smell a whole gallon of blood, just a normal amount." He replied. "Just put a leaf on it to cover it up. After two weeks take the leaf off."

Echo nodded, and walked over to Poppy. "Are you okay?" He asked her. "Was everything good here?" She nodded and smiled. "Nothing to worry about! Well, except Sky. I hope she's okay…"

"She will be!" Grayson shouted from a distance.

"I hope so." Poppy responded, waving her thick white tail near him, and then looking back at Echo.

"I really think we should start thinking about names. I like the name Cedar. Or Oak. I like tree names." She said, amusement sparkling in her big scarlet eyes. "I like Marigold." Echo said. Poppy shrugged. "Okay, maybe." She said.

"AUGHHH." Echo groaned. He was laying on a tall rock, his paws dangling down. It had been three weeks. The pups were coming in just one more.

"What's wrong? Bored?" Willow said. The wolves were hunting again. Echo loved hunting with Willow.

"No, I'm just sick of waiting! I want the pups to come!" Echo yelled, his tail fluffed up. Willow smirked. "Echo, getting tired of waiting is sort of the same as being bored," He said. "It's just one more week, you can survive!"

"Finnnne." Echo said, and sprang up from his rock. "Let's just hunt." The wolves walked off.

"Oh, I have an idea!" Willow said. "It will take your mind off boredom!" Echo's ears perked up. "Remember when I just met you and we did that hunting contest? Let's do it again!" Willow said happily. Echo agreed.

"Ready, set…" He started. "GO!" Willow finished, and ran off.

Echo fled off in the other direction. He was determined to beat Willow this time; Echo felt he needed to prove he was better than the small wolf. After all, he was the *ALPHA*.

Echo ended up with ten rats and a fawn. He wasn't very happy with himself, but he thought he might still have a chance of winning.

He heard Willow's voice shouting in the distance, "FINISHED! FINISHED! Meet at the stream! Meet at the stream!" The voice got louder at the end, so he was obviously already on his way.

Once Echo reached the stream, Willow was already there. He had nine rats in front of him and a mouse. Echo had won.

"Wha…?" Willow mumbled, looking down at his prey and then back at Echo's. "How'd you do that? There's barely any food!" Echo shrugged. "I don't know. I'm just a great hunter, I guess."

Willow's face darkened. Echo could tell he was pretty upset. "Hey..." Echo said considerately.

"You're still a great hunter. You beat me the first time we did this, and you were just a PUP then!" Willow didn't look convinced, but he didn't argue. "Okay..."

Suddenly, Swift quickly ran up to them. "The pups-- they are coming! Come, come, quick!"

Chapter 20

"Poppy?! Are you okay?" Echo yelled once he returned to the dens with Willow and Swift. She raised her head up and forced a small nod.

Echo looked at Grayson. He was experienced with dealing with mothers giving birth; Rona would always demand him to go over and help them.

"She will be okay, it's just a few pups." Grayson said, almost reading Echo's mind, even though he couldn't even see him. Echo exhaled.

"It's okay, Poppy, you are doing great," He said, looking back down at the pretty white wolf. She smiled a bit, and then tiredly put her head back down.

Three pups were born. One was an all brown male with a light brown muzzle, another was a very light gray female with a gray muzzle, and finally a really small pup that was all black. All of them were crying and whimpering except for the tiny black one. Echo wasn't really sure if that one was breathing, but he licked it and hoped for the best.

"What will we name them, Poppy?" Echo said, once all of them calmed down. She closed her eyes, and then quickly opened them. "You choose, I am okay with anything," Poppy finally whispered after a few seconds.

"Okay," Echo said, looking down at the pups again. He pointed at the brown male. "You will be called… Cedar." Echo glanced at Willow. He was smiling brightly.

"You…" Echo said again, this time to the light female. "Will be called Marigold." She let out another small whimper. Finally, Echo turned to the little black pup.

Before saying anything, he looked at Grayson and quietly whispered, "Will this little one be okay?" Grayson put his nose up to the pup and sniffed it. He raised his head back up and frowned. "I… I'm not sure if he will be okay."

Echo carefully felt the little scrap with his paw. It's chest wasn't rising and falling. A shiver went up Echo's spine. *This one is… dead.*

"I… I'm sorry, Poppy," Echo said, tears glazing his eyes. "This one is not okay." Poppy's head jolted up. "He… he won't? Is… he… d-dead?" Echo nodded sadly and looked down at the pup. "I will bury him. Swift and Willow, could you look after the others?" They nodded.

Echo trudged over to a spot and started to dig. He sadly looked down at the lifeless pup and whispered faintly, "I'm sorry. I… love you." And placed him into the small hole, covering it up with some dirt.

"W-well," Poppy said to Echo once he came back. "How are the others?" He looked back at the two pups, who already looked older than they did ten minutes ago. "Fine," Echo responded. "They look very healthy."

Grayson sighed. "I wish I could see them," He said, and felt the scars cutting into his eyes. Sky licked his ear kindly. "They are okay, Grayson." She said. Sky still wanted to be there to see the pups, even though she was still wincing in pain from the gash in her shoulder.

Chestnut was sitting with her own pups, who were getting much older. Crystal looked at the pups. She knew it was her time to take action and ask Echo to train them.

"Echo?" Crystal politely asked, her blue eyes meeting his. "Yes, Crystal? Are you alright?" He responded. She nodded. "Yes, I just, uh…" Crystal didn't know how to ask him.

"Maybe I could train one of the pups…? I mean, could I train one of the pups, please?" She sputtered. Echo blinked in surprise. "W-well…" He said. "Sorry, Crystal, but… you're really young still, and… you don't even know everything about hunting and fighting yet…"

"I actually do," Crystal said, a bit proudly. "Tomorrow, sunrise, I will show you my skills. Meet me at the big oak tree next to the stream." She announced, and trotted away.

"Okay…?" Echo said, and then turned around to sit down next to Poppy. She was curled around the two pups. They couldn't talk or walk, but they had opened their eyes. Marigold's were a brilliant yellow, just like Sunny's. One of Cedar's eyes were brown, and the other one was blue. He let out a little yelp and then fell backwards onto Marigold, who frustratedly squealed back to him and pushed him off. Cedar let out a high-pitched giggle.

"They're so cute…" Poppy said, wrapping her tail around the pups tighter. Marigold let out a sudden yelp, but then snuggled in again. Cedar was still laughing.

"They really are," Echo said, but he was completely thinking about something else. Why did Crystal want to meet him? Why did she say she had skills? Why does she even want to train the pups? Wouldn't that be too much work and stress for a wolf as young as her? Questions, questions, questions. All of which could be answered by Crystal, but Echo wasn't in the mood for talking to her again. He just lay down in front of Poppy and watched her and the pups.

Crystal set out to see Freeze. She needed to talk to him. She was sort of *excited* to talk to him. But one part of Crystal was uncertain. *What if he dies today, anyway? No, no, that can't be it, he said he'd die in a week… but, he also said he would die on the day of the pup's birth… wait, did he? Oh, Freeze, please don't be dead…*

"Crystal?" A hoarse voice rasped. Crystal eagerly turned around to see the scrappy old wolf bundled up next to a rock. She was happy he was alive, but he really didn't look good.

"It is my time now," Freeze whispered. Crystal shook her head. "No, no, please don't die, please…" She said, leaning down and licking him. "Get up, you can do it," Crystal urged, but Freeze didn't budge from his spot.

"I said I would die on the day of the pups. That is what I am doing, small Crystal…" He said quietly. Freeze's eyes started to close, but before he could perish Crystal gave him a swift kick in his leg. Freeze jolted alive.

"Freeze, I don't mean to hurt you, but… please… don't die!" She begged, her blue eyes filled with tears. Freeze dipped his head.

"Goodbye, Crystal. I am sorry." He said, in his old, hoarse voice, and closed his eyes. All the life left his body.

Crystal rested his head on the old gray wolf's ragged fur. It felt cold.

"Goodbye, Freeze…" She said quietly.

"I love you."

Chapter 21

The sun was just rising, and Echo knew he had to go see Crystal. He groaned, and rose up. "Where are you going?" Poppy groggily asked, her pups snuggled up into her. "I have to go talk to Crystal real quick," Echo responded, and quickly padded out of the den.

"You are here, great," Crystal said once Echo found her sitting on a patch of moss near the stream. Echo greeted her.

"What kind of skills did you mean, Crystal? Why did you want to show me?" He asked, immediately after he greeted her.

Crystal showed him everything Freeze taught her. The hunting skills, tracking skills, fighting skills, everything. Echo's ears were curiously perked up the whole time. He was very interested; and impressed.

"How did you learn all this so quickly? You didn't do it on your own, did you?" Echo asked, listening carefully for a response. Crystal tensed. *Should I tell him that **Freeze,** the wolf Echo thought was crazy, taught me all this?* She nervously thought.

"W-well," Crystal finally sputtered after what seemed like a long time. "You know… Freeze… that old wolf we found in the forest? Um… he's the one who taught me. He's actually a really great guy, I promise!"

Echo stared at her, very surprisedly. "He taught

you? But… how…?" He said, frazzled. Crystal explained how she visited Freeze almost every day. The whole time Echo had the same shocked look on his face.

"Okay," Crystal quickly said after she finished telling Echo about her training sessions with Freeze. "So, what do you say? Can I train the new pups?"

Echo hesitated. He thought the small wolf's skills were amazing, almost as good as his own. He really wanted to say yes, but another part of him was unsure. *She's still pretty much a pup too, it would be too much stress,* Echo thought. *But… she seems eager to…*

Echo sighed. "How about…" He started, and Crystal's ears perked up excitedly. "You can, once a week. And then, maybe if your training is really improving them, it could be twice a week, or three times a week, and so on." Echo said. Crystal smiled. "That's great! Thank you so much, Echo! I… I won't let you down!" She chirped, and then ran back to the dens, with Echo following soon after her.

The pups were growing up quickly. Before Echo knew it, they could talk pretty well, and even walk. Echo started to know more about their personalities. Cedar was always mischievous, and liked to fake-battle Marigold. She didn't like his roughhousing. Marigold liked things to be calm and sophisticated.

"Goldie!" Cedar squealed, bouncing up to the pale gray pup. "What d'you want?" Marigold responded, annoyed. "Let's play 'battle' again! Yesterday was so fun!" He chirruped. Marigold groaned. "Battle isn't fun! You always get to be the good wolf, and make me be the evil meanie one!"

Echo laughed. He and Chestnut were watching the pups. "They are adorable, Echo!" She said. "And they are growing up fast. It is hard to believe just a few weeks ago Cedar and Marigold were newborns." Echo nodded in agreement.

"I wonder how Sky is doing," Chestnut said, half to herself. Grayson trotted up and answered, "She is good. It is not infected… well, yet." Echo spotted Skyler sitting in the big den eating some prey.

"Echo, guess what?" Bloodmoon shouted, running up to him. Behind him was Tango, carrying a huge bunch of prey in his mouth.

"We caught 10 prey!" He said happily. Tango spat the prey out next to the big den. He looked slightly annoyed. "I caught 6 and Tango caught only 4!" Bloodmoon boasted. Tango grumbled and walked over to the big den to take a nap.

"Dada?" Cedar said, pawing at Echos leg. "Can me and Goldie go out to hunt?" Echo laughed. "Sorry, Cedar, but you are definitely too young! But you can totally come hunt with me sometime. I could teach you to hunt."

"Okee Dokee! We should soon!" He chirped, and then ran back to Marigold to tell her.

Echo looked around. Swift and Willow were eating a fawn. Sky and Tango were asleep. Chestnut and Grayson were talking. The pups were playing. Echo didn't see Crystal.

"Crystal?" Echo yelled. Swift swung his head over to him. "She went hunting with Tango and Bloodmoon. You should ask them." He said.

"Bloodmoon, where is Crystal?" Echo asked, running up to him. Bloodmoon shrugged. "I dunno. She went hunting with us, but on the way back she must've wandered off or something." He said truthfully.

"I'm going to look for her." Echo announced and walked away.

"CRRYYYYSTTTAL!" Echo shouted, walking through the forest. "Yes?" Crystal responded, trotting out from behind a rock. "Why are you here? What have you been doing?" He frantically said.

"I… I..." Crystal stuttered. "Was sitting with… um… F-Freeze..."

Echo sighed. He knew that the small wolf missed her wise, old mentor, but she still needed to pay attention to the pack. "I promise I'll go in a minute," Crystal said, almost reading his mind. Echo nodded. "A minute," He repeated, padding away.

"Didja find her?" Bloodmoon asked once Echo returned. He nodded, but before the tiny gray wolf

114

could say a word, Echo walked into his den. Poppy was there.

"Hi, dear," Echo said, sitting on the ground to settle down. "Hello…" She mumbled. Poppy almost looked a bit upset.

"What's up?" He asked kindly. Poppy just shrugged and rested her head on her paws. That didn't really answer any of Echo's questions.

After a few minutes of nagging, Echo finally got it out of her. "It's just… you know how our little pup died? I've just been thinking about him, and… It's really selfish, but… I want him back. I feel like we should of done more to keep him alive, instead of just calling him dead and burying him."

Echo shook his head frantically. "Poppy, you are not selfish one bit! I too wish that I didn't just except his death. But… what do we do about it now? UNbury him?"

Poppy hesitated, and looked at her paws. Finally, she answered, "I guess. Maybe Grayson could do something about him, like pump life back into him or something. Ugh, I bet it's too late for that, though…." She trailed off.

"But we can still try, it's worth a shot," Echo quickly replied, smiling a little bit. "Let's do it now, before Grayson goes to sleep," He said. "Hopefully he is done with caring for Sky and her shoulder," Poppy said, running after the Alpha.

"Yes?" Grayson asked, sitting down on his squishy grass bed, inspecting a herb's smell.

"Well… it seems stupid now, but me and Echo were wondering if you could bring this guy back to life…" Poppy muttered, awkwardly placing the lifeless pup on his paws. The gray-brown wolf lowered his head to sniff the pup. It's fur ruffled.

"I'm sorry, but… I do not think I'm skilled enough to bring a pup back to life. I can only heal minor wounds." Grayson said, his cloudy scratched eyes staring down at the pup, rather than Poppy or Echo.

"O-oh… well, that's okay, Grayson. Good night…" Echo said, lowering his head to pick up the pup.

"WAIT!" Grayson shouted, holding the pup down. "I think I have an idea! Fetch me some lilacs, I recall my cousin once told me they bring energy! Maybe if we give him a whole bunch of them, then… the pup might live!" Both of the wolves ran off to fetch a whole bunch of the small purple flowers.

Chapter 22

"Ugh, daddy, what are you doing? It's so late and you are making a ruckus!" Cedar complained, trotting into the big den. When the small pup saw the three wolves force-feeding the pup flowers, he stopped. "Who IS that?" He squeaked.

"This is your brother, Cedar," Poppy quickly shouted, continuing to help the pup chew the flowers.

Cedar lit up. "A BROTHER?!" He happily screamed, trembling with excitement. Skyler, who was asleep next to Grayson, woke up with a groan. Echo shushed Cedar.

Suddenly, the little black pup coughed up a bit of blood. "HE IS ALIVE!" Echo announced, waking up the rest of the pack. "Oops," He whispered, but it was too late. Everyone was crowded around him, Grayson, and Poppy, asking him questions. "Who?" "What?" "Where?"

"Uuuuurgh..." the pup groaned, before closing his eyes again. "He needs something for strength! Quick, get some... ferns! I think ferns are good for strength!" Grayson yelled.

As quick as a cheetah, Poppy barreled outside to gather the ferns. The pup whimpered again. "Shh, it's okay, don't try to speak," Echo whispered, lightly pressing his muzzle against the little scrap's head. "Wh-who?" the pup responded in a small voice. "Shh!" Echo demanded.

"I got the ferns!" Poppy yelled, running up to the wolves. "Hi, little buddy," She said to the tiny pup. "I'm your mama! Here, eat these, they will make you feel much better. They are a bit bitter, but I know you can handle it!" The pup chomped up the ferns.

"GAG! Pleh! Yucky!" He squealed, spitting little bits of the fern everywhere. "Nononononono," Poppy said, collecting all the pieces of fern and putting them back in his mouth. The pup gagged a bit, but finally swallowed them.

"Do you feel better? Strong?" Echo asked, smiling at the little pup. Without answering his question, the pup responded, "Are you my dada? Who is I called?"

Echo looked at Poppy. Maybe she knew a name. Luckily, she did. "Smoke?" Poppy whispered. *Good name!* Echo mouthed out, and then looked back at the pup.

"I am your dada, and your name is Smoke." Echo said, wrapping his tail a little more around Smoke. He yawned. "I… sleep...." Smoke murmured, and then fell into deep sleep, resting on Echo's tail.

"You can go back to your den with Marigold. I bet she would be scared if she woke up and you guys weren't there." Grayson suggested. "I agree," Poppy said, looking at Echo. He nodded, and picked up Smoke by the scruff. Poppy did the same with Cedar, who also fell asleep.

"Okay, Smokey," Marigold said. It was a week after Smoke had woken up. "If you are going to be our brother, you need to follow our rules!" She demanded.

Cedar rolled his eyes. "Ugh, Goldie, you're no fun. You should let Smokey have a GOOD TIME!" He chirped. Smoke blinked.

"I don't care, you can gimme rules," Smoke whispered. "I owe you a whole lot for waking me up!"

Echo smiled. He loved watching his pups play. The time between his pups being born and Crystal, Tango, and Bloodmoon growing up was a time where he barely got to see cute pups play-fighting or talking with each other.

Cedar let out a loud sigh. "Nobody here is fun! I want more pups to play with!" He shouted.

Suddenly, Sky emerged from the den. Her shoulder still looked bad, but it was getting better. "You will be." She announced proudly.

Echo's eyes almost popped out of his head.

"REALLY?!" He asked, running in front of Skyler. "You're pregnant? Oh my goodness!" Echo yelled. She nodded. "I already have names. One for girl, one for a boy."

"Pebble for the boy, Maple for the girl," Grayson said, trotting out of the den behind her. "Hopefully we have two pups."

"When are you having them? Two months?" Echo asked. Skyler embarrassedly shuffled her paws."One month. I… didn't really realise until last week." She mumbled.

"Only a month!?" Cedar screeched in surprise. "Awesome! So many fun new friends!"

Smoke looked at his paws, and Marigold rolled her eyes.

"Be nice to your siblings," Echo demanded, and Cedar sighed and nodded. "I'm just glad that I'm getting new pups to play with..." He grumbled, stomping away.

"I wish that I could see them. I wish that I could see all the pups." Grayson sighed, flicking his tail at Tango, sitting faraway eating prey. He noticed and growled. "I'm no pup! I'm plenty big now. I'm bigger than Bloodmoon!"

Echo took a quick glance at Bloodmoon, who didn't seem to hear. He looked a bit tired. And skinny. Was he okay?

Bloodmoon slowly turned his head towards Echo. He didn't want to admit it, but Echo flinched a little bit when he saw Bloodmoon's eyes meet his; they were not the usual mint-green eyes; they looked cloudy and gray.

"What are *YOU* looking at?" Bloodmoon angrily rasped. Echo stepped back. Bloodmoon had never, ever been this bad tempered. His fur was ruffled and dirty and stood on end. He was trembling the slightest bit.

"A-are you okay?" Echo nervously asked. Bloodmoon's face darkened. He didn't say a word. After a minute of silence, he trudged back in the den and slumped down on his bed in the corner.

"I'll look at him," Grayson suggested, flicking his bushy tail towards Bloodmoon. "Well, smell him."

The next three hours, Echo, Tango, Crystal, Chestnut, and Swift anxiously waited to hear what Grayson had to say about Bloodmoon.

"What if he's *not* okay?" Tango asked, his voice trembling the slightest bit. Everyone hesitated.

"He will be okay!" Swift reassured, but he didn't look completely confident.

"I really don't know," Grayson announced, padding sadly out of the big den. "I'm definitely not perfect at this caring for the sick stuff. I told Bloodmoon to rest, but he wouldn't listen. He didn't have any lumps or anything. He smelled… dirty. I think he is upset about something." He explained.

But… what? Echo thought.

Chapter 23

Echo sighed. He had been curled up in his bed for almost two hours now; but he still couldn't find sleep. So much seemed to be going on; Skyler's pups, Bloodmoon being upset, none of the pups getting along… Echo needed a break. Being the Alpha was hard.

Poppy started to stir in her sleep. Echo placed his tail on her back, and she stopped. The pups were all spread out around the den. Bloodmoon used to sleep in Echo's den, but he stopped a few days ago. He thought he was old enough.

"Echo," Poppy whispered groggily. She must've still woken up, even after Echo tried to calm her down.

"Go back to sleep." She demanded. Echo shrugged. "I don't know. I… can't. I just have so much to think about; raising our pups, keeping our pack safe, taking care of Bloodmoon… Bloodmoon. I hope he's okay…" He whispered, shaking his head sadly. "I… ugh."

Poppy gave Echo a sympathetic look. "Everything will be okay, Echo. The pups will be born soon. After that, Cedar, Smoke, and Marigold will have new friends. Chestnut and Swift's pups will be able to take care of themselves. Bloodmoon will definitely recover. After that, you'll be fine!"

Echo felt like he was waiting for his own pups all over again. The next days were filled with sighing, groaning, not knowing what to do. Cedar stopped paying attention to Marigold, and started trying to persuade Smoke to be as 'cool' as he was. Bloodmoon was stayed in bed a lot, and the times he came out, all he did was eat. Skyler, Grayson, Willow, Chestnut, Poppy, and Swift all waited along with Echo, sometimes going hunting. Tango and Crystal were the only ones who were always doing something. Every day they would hunt, clean, bring food to Bloodmoon, Cedar, Marigold, and Smoke. Echo's pups had stopped needing Poppy's milk.

"One more day!" Chestnut announced, waddling out of the den on her stumpy brown legs.

Grayson followed her, looking as proud a ever. He was going to be a father. *Hopefully being a dad isn't hard...* He nervously thought.

"Oh my goodness, Oh my goodness," Sky wailed in the middle of the night. Grayson sprang up; he knew what was coming. "It's the pups!"

Grayson let out a quick howl to alert his pack. They got up, eyes still drooping, and trudged over to Skyler. When everyone realised she was having her pups, they immediately became one hundred percent awake.

Grayson could barely keep himself contained. He was squealing in excitement, but he managed to keep his squeaking quiet so he wouldn't hurt Sky's ears.

Skyler let out a howl. The first pup was being born. At first, Grayson couldn't tell what gender it was. It smelled exactly like Skyler. Quickly, he bent down to give it a quick sniff. It was a male.

Suddenly, Sky went limp.

"SKYLER!" Grayson screamed, immediately noticing his mate not breathing.

Quickly, she jolted awake. "I-is it over?" She murmured, her hoarse voiced shaking. "It is, dear, I think you only had one. A male." Grayson answered, leaning down to lick his son. The pup squealed a little bit, but then fell asleep.

"What color is he?" Grayson asked Echo, who was watching the small pup in awe. "Grayish-brown with a light gray muzzle," Echo responded. Grayson eagerly wanted the pup to open their eyes so Echo could tell him which color they were.

It was late in the morning when the pup opened up his eyes. His eyes were a beautiful blue exactly like Skyler's. The moment he opened his eyes, Cedar ran up to him.

"You can talk now, right?" He asked, bouncing up and down. The pup nodded slowly. "I... think so..." He squeaked. Pups always learned to talk quickly.

"Good. right now, we are going to run away to hunt! Don't tell papa- well, for you, it's Echo, I guess!" Cedar squeaked. The pup looked a bit hesitant. "I don't even have a name yet. Maybe, first, mama can name me, and then we can go."

"A name, yes," Grayson said, padding up behind the little gray-brown pup. "Your name will be Pebble." He said. "And, Cedar, pups aren't allowed deep in the forest unless they're training."

"FIIIINE!" He grumbled, trotting away. Cedar seemed to be turning into a really disrespectful pup, which would most likely lead to being a disrespectful wolf, and that worried Echo. He thought his kin would be at least a little bit like him; gentle, sweet, a good leader. At least Cedar was brave.

"He's gone?" Cedar whispered to Pebble, who was standing on unsteady paws, staring deep into the forest.

"Yeah, why?" Pebble asked, turning to Cedar. "We're gonna sneak out and catch prey, duh!" He responded, whipping his tail quickly against the small pup. Pebble stumbled a bit.

Once he got back on his four paws, he pointed out, "But… papa told us not to." Cedar rolled his eyes. "Grayson is a boring-butt!" He announced. Pebble let out a quick gasp. "GRAYSON IS MY PAPA!" He screamed, and pounced onto Cedar, biting his next. Cedar screeched. *This isn't play! This isn't play! Stop!*

"Nobody calls my papa a butt!" Pebble yelled, rolling across the grassy floor on top of Cedar.

"Break it up!" Echo yelled, picking up Cedar by the scruff. Grayson ran over and picked up Pebble.

"What's going on? Were they fighting?" He asked.
"Yeah," Echo said, biting a bit harder down on
Cedar's scruff.

"He hurts me, I hurt him!" Cedar yowled, kicking
his back legs into Echo's legs. Echo's jaw flung
open as he let out a small yowl, sending Cedar
falling onto the ground. The pup shot towards
Pebble. The pup screeched as Cedar scratched his
hind leg. Scarlet blood dripped down. Pebble was
wailing.

Chapter 24

Skyler came rushing out, and swooped up her pup. "Who did this to you?" She nervously asked, but Pebble couldn't answer. He was still crying. Sky looked over at Echo, then Grayson.

"Cedar," Echo said, narrowing his eyes angrily at his pup. "Cedar did it. I'm sorry, I'll talk to him," Echo said, firmly grasping his pup by the scruff.

"Okay…" Sky said, giving Cedar a quick glare, before trotting away with Pebble.

"CEDAR!" Echo scolded once they got into the den. Luckily, Poppy was teaching Marigold some hunting moves near the stream, and Smoke was watching Tango and Crystal show him how to fight.

"Pebble is only about a day old, and you are MUCH bigger and stronger. You should have nev-" "But he hurt me more!" Cedar protested, interrupting his father. Echo growled. "That is no excuse. You must apologize to him, Grayson, and Skyler. Do you understand?" He asked, his eyes still glimmering with anger.

Cedar grumbled, not saying a word. "DO YOU UNDERSTAND?" Echo repeated, his voice rising with furiousness.

Suddenly, the pup ran. He ran out of the den, into the forest, his legs stamping rapidly against the ground.

"CEDAR!" Echo yelled, barreling after the pup. After twenty minutes of looking and looking, no one could find him.

Echo sat down on the grassy ground. He had lost hope. There was no way he was going to find his son. *He might even be DEAD by now,* Echo thought, a shiver running down his spine. Cedar may have been a troublemaker, but Echo still would always love him.

J-just a bit longer! Echo yelled in his head, running around the forest, sniffing everything wildly to just find a trace of Cedar's scent.

After five more minutes, Echo spotted some blood splattered on the ground. He nervously crouched down to smell it. It was Cedar's

"NO!" Echo pleaded, looking up into the sky. "Don't be dead! You can't let him be dead!"

He looked up to see Cedar's body, above it a shadow, who's claws looked drenched in blood. The shadow looked no bigger than Marigold.

"Stop! Murderer!" Echo yelled, running over to the wolf. But he stopped once he saw what it looked like.

A small, very light gray, yellowish green eyed pup. "Greetings," He squeaked. "Do you know this pup? He wandered into the forest and I think he got hurt. I was checking if he was okay."

"That's... my son... you... didn't kill him, did you?" Echo asked, looking down at Cedar. To his surprise, Cedar was breathing, but his breaths were slow.

"No," the light gray pup said. "Definitely not. He isn't even dead. Just really hurt. Look," He put his paw on a giant wound on Cedar's back. "I think it was one of the gorilla hogs. One of the *hunter* gorilla hogs."

Echo looked back down at his son. He rested his head on Cedar's fur. "Be okay, please, be okay…" He said, his eyes squeezed shut.

"My name is Chee," The pup said, trying to change the subject. "And I am proud to be Breezy's nephew! He the great wolf who got stolen by gorilla hogs. I was just looking for him… when I found him. He was dead." Chee stared ahead, surprisingly not looking sad or disappointed at all by his Uncle's death.

"Well, If you don't have a home, want to join my pack?" Chee's eyes brightened. "Oh, yes, definitely! More wolves to… p-play with!" He said cheerfully. "Great! Follow me," Echo said, picking up Cedar.

"*Chee?*" Swift snickered a little bit. Chestnut nudged him. "Hi, Chee, welcome!" She said. "Hi," Skyler said. "Hello." Grayson said. "What's up?" Willow said. "Hi there!" The pups chirped. "Hey," Tango and Crystal said. Bloodmoon stayed quiet.

"He looks like Freeze," Crystal said. Echo looked at her. "I… think he's Freeze's nephew." Echo said to her. Crystals ears perked up and she ran to Chee.

"Welcome, Hi, hi! How are you?" Chee stepped back a bit. "Well, I'm doing pretty good. Except for getting lost in a random forest and then realising my uncle is dead."

Cedar raised his head a bit. He was awake. "You!" He yowled, glaring at the light gray pup. "You almost killed me!" Chee's eyes widened. "He must've thought it was me. B-but it wasn't." He nervously said.

"IT WAS!" Cedar screeched.

"I'll put him back to sleep," Poppy said, carrying Cedar by the scruff into the den.

"Well, um, I'm going to go hunt for a little bit. Bye!" Chee announced, turning around for the forest. Suddenly, his ears perked. "Maybe Pebble can come with me so I can show him the forest for the first time!"

Echo thought that was a pretty good idea, but Skyler looked uncertain.

"I guess," She said, looking down at Pebble, who was sitting at her paws. "What do you think, Pebble?"

"I wanna!" The pup chirped, waving his paws in the air.

"Lets go!" Chee said, beckoning the pup to him with his tail.

"I hope they're okay," Sky whispered in Echo's ear once Chee left with Pebble. "Chee sounds responsible, but I just feel... nervous... sending my pup with someone I just met."

Echo shrugged. "I assume everything will be okay. It's natural for a new mother to be nervous for her pups."

It had been three hours, and the pups still haven't returned. Sky was frantic.

"Oh my goodness, what if something happened to them? It usually only takes an hour to hunt!" She yelled. Echo rested his tail on her shoulder.

"Everything will be fine, promise," Echo reassured her. "They must just be having trouble finding prey."

All of a sudden, a scream was heard in the distance. It was Pebble.

"PEBBLE!" Skyler yelled, speeding into the forest, as fast as a cheetah. Echo followed after her. "WILLOW, YOU'RE IN CHARGE!" he yelled behind him.

"Pebble? Chee?" Echo said, looking around the forest. "He's... he's..." Chee stuttered, looking down at Pebble, who lay unconscious on the ground.

Blood was splattered all over the leaves. "It was, um, a black and white wolf, with... um, b-blue eyes. I-I think."

"NO! PEBBLE!" Skyler screamed once she saw her dead son on the ground. "You..." She looked up at Chee. "You! You never take care of him! I knew you were bad news! You shouldn't of let those evil wolves murder him!"

Chee's eyes grew big and innocent. "I… I… didn't mean to! Sniffle…" He started to cry, but it didn't sound like crying. It sounded like wailing mixed with sneezing.

"Let's just take these guys back to the dens," Echo said, nudging Chee. He got up slowly. Sky picked up Pebble, tears still glazing her eyes.

"What happ-" Grayson started to say, but he got interrupted by Chestnut. "P-P-P-PEBBLE!" She said loudly, running up to Skyler and Echo.

"He's dead," Sky grumbled, still glaring at Chee. "Pebble is dead?!" Grayson yelled, running up to Pebble's lifeless body in Skyler's jaws.

"I will bury him." Willow announced, walking up to touch the pup's fur with his nose. "Although he lived a short life, this pup had a good one. He would have been a wonderful fighter."

Echo was proud of Willow's speech. He felt so glad that Willow had grown up into a brave, mighty wolf. He would be a good Alpha.

Willow leaned forward to take Pebble from Skyler's jaws. He walked away to the place where Smoke was buried.

That night, Echo couldn't sleep. He didn't know what to do about Chee. Echo had to admit; he didn't want this pup in the pack. But… how would he tell Chee that?

Chapter 25

"Chee," Echo said. He was having a private talk with the pup near the gorilla hog town. "You seem like a responsible pup, but I can't let you be in the pack anymore."

"WHAT?" The pup yelled. "But... why?!"

"I know, this might just seem like a coincidence, but... ever since you came into our pack, then bad things have been happening. Cedar is injured, Pebble is dead, and Skyler is sad all th-" "But... but... I..." Chee interrupted in protest.

"I don't care." Echo said, a bit more firm. "I, and most of the pack, are convinced you killed Pebble. Those blood marks all over the leaves must have been you trying to wipe the blood off your paws. Get out of my territory!" He snarled.

"I will be back, Echo," Chee announced, growling. "I will be back to wreak havoc on your pack."

Chee ran into the forest, his thin tail waving behind him. His fur was ruffled up in anger.

"Did you finally get rid of that brat?" Skyler asked once Echo returned. "Yes," He said, but he wasn't completely sure that he did.

"Good," Grayson said, trotting up behind Skyler. "Our pack is a good size anyway. It doesn't have to be as big as Rona's." Echo agreed. "I think we're safe... for now."

"It's finally over," Poppy sighed as she laid next to Echo. It had been a few weeks since Chee had left, and luckily, there had been no scent of him anywhere.

"What?" Echo asked. "The craziness. The pup palooza, Chee, that old furball you found in the forest... It's all over. The forest is peaceful." Poppy responded, wrapping her tail over her paws. "We can relax." She whispered, and drifted off to sleep.

For the first time in a while, Echo thought the same. Nothing bad was happening. The forest was full of prey. Everyone was safe. Cedar was better. But Echo realised with a shiver...

When everything's right, something wrong is bound to happen.

"Anything bad going on?" Echo asked once Swift, Willow, and Chestnut returned from hunting. It was the early morning. "We saw three dogs. They all had collars. One was black and white, one was brown, and one was grey. They all had blood-red collars." Chestnut reported. "One was a girl. The black and white one." Willow added.

"Okay, that's not too bad," Echo said. "We just need to fight back if they start to steal our prey or make their own dens on our territory."

"Did they see you?" Poppy asked, walking out of her den. "Only the girl did." Chestnut answered, but she still looked nervous. "We should probably do something. I'll talk to her, if you'd like." She said.

"You really want to?"

"Yeah."

"Want someone to come with you?"

"I think I can handle it. All I do for the pack is hunt, I want to do something bigger."

"Okay. Stay safe."

Chestnut spun around and trotted into the forest. She felt ready. She felt proud. She felt strong, even with her relatively dull teeth and flat claws.

Luckily, the girl was alone. She was setting up a bed made of wet leaves. Three beds, actually.

She sniffed the air, and looked around. The dog finally glanced at Chestnut. Her fur bristled. Her cover was blown.

"Are you spying on me?" she spat, her eyes narrowed into slits. Chestnut stepped out. "No, no," she said, in her calmest voice. "It's just-- my pack, I mean, Echo's pack, lives near here, and this is sort of… on our territory…" Her voice trailed off with nervousness. How would the dog respond?

"Oh, I see," she said, turning her head, her eyes still fixed on Chestnut. "You live *near* here and now every bit of land in this forest is yours." Her claws slowly poked out through her fur.

"I'm sorry. But we would really appreciate it if you were just to move a little bit. That open field, perhaps? It's very big. Lots of land. A-and, you can own i-"

"Are you trying to bribe me?" The dog interrupted. "N-no! I was just-" "Nobody bribes me, Speckle, or my servants, Rat and Mold. we could rip you to shreds. Oh, and we can't forget Scrape, our new addition. Found him in *this* forest. He said this was *his* forest. You're the one who should be scrammin'!"

"Scrape?" Chestnut repeated. "Scrape! You know him?" Speckle asked. "I... don't know," Chestnut responded, shuffling her paws.

"My name is Chestnut," She said, trying to change the subject so she couldn't talk about her servants more.

"I don't care what your name is! SHOO!" Speckle yowled. Chestnut sighed, and trotted away. Although she discovered new things about the dogs, she still felt defeated.

"Speckle. Rat. Mold. Scrape." Swift said, padding anxiously around the den.

"Quit pacing! I'm trying to get some rest!" Bloodmoon spat, his fur fluffing out with annoyance. "Sorry," Swift whispered back to him.

"Yeah," Chestnut said to Swift. "Those are their names." He nodded. "Well, by the way you described them, they seem no-nonsense... and, well, bad-tempered. But... there's only four of them, and there's twelve of us. I think we can take them."

"The pups can't fight," Chestnut pointed out. "So, only nine of us. Tango and Crystal will be ready, I think."

"Oh, and Skyler," Swift said, disappointed. "Her shoulder still isn't healed. She's probably out."

"Eight." Chestnut said, looking at her paws. "But that's still double what they have…"

"We can still do it, hopefully," Swift said to her, licking her ear. "It'll be fine. I bet they just act tough on the outside."

"I still don't understand why animals become… well, rude. I would never want to be rude. What type of parents would want to make their child rude? How were they raised?" Chestnut asked, her claws starting to stick out more. Swift put his paw on her back, signalling her to calm down. Chestnut sighed and rested her head on her paws.

How were they raised?

Chapter 26

"Mommy, I'm sick of sitting here in this cage. Can we go now?" The pup asked. The mother sighed. "It's not as simple as that, Fuzzy. I wish we could go, but first we need to get adopted. Or... or..." She trailed off, not wanting to upset her pup. But the mother knew she would have to tell Fuzzy sometime.

"Another human is coming by!" Fuzzy yelped happily, swinging her head over to the wire wall of the cage.

"It's a cub! Human cubs always want puppies, Fuzzy. Act cute!" The mother said, nudging Fuzzy. "Wait, but will they get you, too?" she asked her mother. The mother didn't answer.

"It's a puppy! A little dalmatian!" the cub squealed, picking up Fuzzy. "No! Mommy!" she yelled as the cub pulled her away. "Don't be afraid! You'll be okay!" the mother said back. "Goodbye, sweetness..."

"You're stuck here now too, ey?" another pup said to Fuzzy once she arrived at the cub's home. "Yeah," she said. The pup sighed. "At least they feed us. It's better than the pound," he said.

"Is that where I just came from?" Fuzzy asked, curiosity and excitement flowing through her. How much did this pup know? He needed to tell her everything about everything!"

"Yep. You're lucky you didn't get killed. I bet your mom did. My mom did," the pup answered. Fuzzy was about to disagree, but the pup changed the subject.

"ANYWAY, my name is George, but that's a lame name and I'd rather be called Mold. Call me Mold." He said. "I'm Fuzzy." Fuzzy mumbled, suddenly feeling embarrassed about her name. "I don't care. I'm gonna call you Speckle, 'cause you're covered in black specks." Mold said.

"Who's that?" Fuzzy asked, spinning around to face a dark brown pup. "That's Timothy, but call him Rat or he'll rip your ears off." Mold said.

"Hey," Rat rasped. His voice made him sound like an old dying dog, but he looked like a pup. "Mold- I have an idea to escape this dump and live in the fo... fo..." "Forest," Fuzzy said. "Don't correct me!" Rat demanded. Mold's ears perked up.

"A plan? Tell me, tell me!" Mold begged. Rat opened his mouth, but suddenly glared at Fuzzy and then leaned in closer and whispered something in Mold's ears. "Ooooh!" He said. "Let's try it!"

Fuzzy stayed quiet for the whole day until night. "Now's our chance!" Mold squeaked in Rat's ear. "It's dark, so they won't notice!" Suddenly, Mold wailed. The cub went running.

"What's wrong, Georgie?" she said. Mold scratched at the door. "Oh, you have to pee," the cub giggled, opening the door. Rat went out too. Fuzzy, not knowing what to do, followed after. "Aw, Timmy and Sally have to go too," she said. *Sally? Is that what she's calling ME?* Fuzzy thought, still following the pups.

"It's chilly," she finally said, after following them all the way to the edge of the fence.

"What? Why are you here? Scram!" Rat yowled. Mold scratched him. "You can come with us, I guess. But you're so small I bet you'll die from the cold! Heehee!" he barked, running swiftly out a hole in the fence, with Rat following closely. Fuzzy yelped and tried to catch up.

"Where are we?" Fuzzy finally managed to whisper. They had been travelling forever, and she had been out of breath the whole entire time.

"The *forest*," Mold said. Fuzzy looked around. She was in the middle of a field of tall, dark things. The ground was strangely squishy, and the tall dark things felt rough. "What are these? What's this? Why does it feel like that?"

"That's trees, that's grass, and they feel like that 'cause they're plants!" Rat answered. "Now, shush."

"This is where we will sleep." Mold said, pointing paw to a patch of long smushed down grass. It was obvious Mold was the boss.

"What's that?" Rat rasped, his nose tingling. Suddenly, a wave of utterly disgusting air flew through Fuzzy's nostrils. "Ew!"

"I think it's a bear!" Mold yelled. "What's a b-bear?" Fuzzy asked nervously. "Oh my gosh, Speckle, are you an IDIOT?!" Rat screamed in Fuzzy's face. *O-oh yeah, my name is Speckle now,* she thought. "S-sorry…" Speckle whispered.

"It is!" Mold yowled, his eyes growing wide. Speckle turned around to see a huge, furry brown monster stepping up to them, it's claws outstretched.

Rat growled loudly and sprung at the bear. With one swipe of it's paw, the bear flung Rat into one of the tall trees. He groaned, and fell against the grass, blood trickling from the spot the bear hit him. Mold's eyes grew wide.

"NO! NOT RAT!" he screeched, barrelling up to the bear, swiping across his face. Three long scars were plastered on the bear's cheek. It lunged down onto Mold, biting his hind leg. It came straight off. The pup went limp onto the ground.

Suddenly, Speckle started to burn with fury. She had never felt this way ever, and the first time she did was for two pups that weren't even that nice to her. A growl rumbled loud in her throat as she jumped onto the bears face, scraping her claws against its eyes. It fell over, blinded.

The bear let out a quick roar and then ran off into the distance. For the first time ever, Speckle felt strong.

"Mold?" She asked nervously, spinning over to him. Speckle pressed her nuzzle against him, and luckily, he was still breathing. She let out a sigh of relief.

Rat stood up, his legs trembling. "You... saved us..." He said quietly. "I-is Mold okay?"

"Yes..." a voice murmured. It was Mold. "Thank you so, so much, Speckle. You saved our lives. If there is anything we can do for you, we will do it. I'll even be your servant." Mold said, unsteadily standing up on his three remaining legs. "Me too," Rat added quickly.

Speckle's eyes glimmered with satisfaction. Finally, she was content. She felt stronger then ever. She finally felt happy.

But... was it really worth it?

Chapter 27

"Hello. By what I have heard from Chestnut, you are Speckle, Mold, and Rat." Echo said, sitting in front of the three dogs. Mold and Rat looked intimidated by Echo's size, but Speckle sat tall, her chin up.

"That's right. But there's no time for questions. What're you doing on our territory?" Speckle asked, her eyes angry slits.

"That's the problem." Echo answered calmly, doing everything he could to tell Speckle that this was *his* territory, without upsetting her.

"You think that this is your territory. But… it's not. Me and my pack have lived here much longer. It's not fair for you to just waltz in and call it yours."

Speckle's eyes widened slightly. She obviously didn't have a comeback. "Scrape will be back soon," She said, changing the subject. "He won't like to see you here."

Echo raised his eyebrow. "I'd like to meet this 'Scrape,' if that's okay." He said back. Speckle rolled her eyes. "Fine." She said, padding away to her bed.

"Wait!" Rat said. "Actually, we went to another forest when we were just pups, and that was our forest, and then we were travelling across the forest for a long long long time, and we came here, and set up our den here. So technically this is still our forest!" He pointed out.

"You can't own a whole forest. You can own small territories, but not a whole forest. I think it would be much easier for everyone if you just went back to your old territory. The territory that is actually *yours.*" Echo responded.

"Maybe we will, maybe we won't!" Speckle said. "Scrape will need to agree!"

"What did you say about me?" An unusually high voice said angrily. A small gray pup padded out behind a big rock. It was Chee.

"You!" He said, snarling. Echo took a step back. "Echo! I told you I'd be back, and I am! Guys, attack!" The dogs all jumped on Echo, scratching, biting, snarling. He could barely see what was going on; every time Echo was about to fight back, someone else jumped on him.

"ENOUGH!" Echo yelled, sending all the dogs skidding onto the ground.

"You need to leave. You need to." He said. "My pack is bigger than yours. And they will gladly fight."

"We will." A familiar voice said. To Echo's surprise, it was Bloodmoon. "I knew something was wrong from the beginning. That's why I was so upset. I will never be happy again until you get out of here, you grubs!"

He lunged at Chee, biting the small pup's neck. The pup yowled and waved his paws wildly, trying to scratch, but failing. Then, Chee died. His yowls turned into to blood gurgling through his throat, and he went limp onto the ground. He was dead.

Speckle's ears perked up, and she scratched Bloodmoon across the face. In this fight, Bloodmoon was weaker. Speckle bit hard down on the small wolf's neck. He screeched. Everything seemed to be going on the same way that the fight with Chee went. Bloodmoon was about to die.

"STOP!" Echo begged, slashing his paw against Speckle's legs, knocking her onto the ground. She growled. Then, Rat and Mold jumped out, attacking Bloodmoon. Before Echo could do anything to save him, Bloodmoon was gone. All the fury in Echo's body spilled out.

After about fifteen minutes, Rat and Mold were dead. Speckle ran away, far, far, away, yowling the whole time.

"No… no… no…" Crystal repeated, her head hanging down to look at her paws. "Bloodmoon can't be dead… he can't… I loved him…" Swift licked her ear. "It's okay… Chee is dead. So is Rat and Mold." Everything Swift said still couldn't make her feel better.

"Alright, Cedar, Smoke, and Marigold," Crystal said, waving her tail to signal the pups to line up. It had been a week since Bloodmoon's death. Crystal had started to get over it, though a pit was still in her stomach.

"Can we do something fun today?" Cedar asked, his big eyes hopeful. "May we!" Marigold corrected. Cedar gave her a quick dirty look but then turned his head back to Crystal.

"You'll see," Crystal replied with a small smile. "But before that, I need to tell you guys something." All of the pup's ears perked up.

"I think that you guys have been doing very good in your training, and in a while, you won't need me." Suddenly, a rush of pride went through Crystal. Guiding the pups had been a great experience, and she still couldn't thank Echo enough.

"What?" Smoke squeaked. He was smaller than all the others, and had a bit of trouble catching up. "I'm not ready! I'm still really tiny!"

"It's okay, Smoke," Crystal said kindly. "I'll train you for about a week more than these guys. And remember, if you ever want to ask me about anything, hunting, fighting, or anything, you can, and I will be glad to teach you."

"I for one can't wait!" Cedar squealed. "I'm gonna have a real part in the pack! I will be able to fight and hunt on my own! Mama won't tell me I can't! Haha!" Marigold was smiling, too. "Me too. But I will miss fake-fighting with Cedar while you critique us. I love that…"

"Aw, it's okay, Goldie," Crystal said. "You'll see me every day. I'm in your pack!"

"What are we gonna do today?!" Cedar yelpped excitedly. "We are going to travel," Crystal replied. "I asked Poppy if I could take you to the open field, and she said yes. She even said we could stay for the night, but only if I took great care of you. I agreed." Cedar screeched loudly in delight, and Marigold let out a happy little bark, but Smoke looked nervous.

"Isn't it *dangerous?*" He mumbled, trembling. Crystal gave him a quick lick on the head. "Poppy said that she really trusted me. You'll be safe, Smoke." He hesitated, but then nodded slowly.

"We're leaving in about an hour," Crystal said. "AN HOUR?!" Cedar echoed loudly. "That's so close to now!" He squealed. "I can't wait!"

"Okay, you can take a piece of prey to start off with, and have some ferns for strength, and I think that these berries are good for sore paws because I rubbed them on my paws once when I was hunting and they helped…" Poppy said frantically, pushing berries and prey towards them. It was right before they were going to travel, and the pups couldn't wait.

Chapter 28

"We'll be fine, I promise," Crystal said. "I'm not a pup anymore!" Poppy nodded, but she still looked a bit unsure.

"And we're off!" Crystal announced, padding out of the den, Marigold and Smoke huddled to her side and Cedar running in front of them.

"Can we hunt? I'm hungry, and Smoke keeps whimpering so I think he's hungry too!" Cedar chirped once they were near the place Bloodmoon had died.

"Just a little longer, we're not even at the stream yet! After we cross it, you'll be even more hungry." Crystal said.

"CROSS THE STREAM?!" Smoke yelled, his eyes widening with fear. "I'll carry you over it…" Crystal said, but shivered at the thought of wading through the icy water with three pups on her back. She wasn't even fully grown yet.

"There it is!" Marigold said, hopping over to the stream. "And lookit that fish!" She waved her paw toward a small guppy swimming. "Can we catch it? Pleeease? Mama told me that fish tasted good!"

"Maybe," Crystal lied, but the last thing she wanted to do was try and catch a fish while swimming through the freezing narrow river.

She picked up Smoke, then Marigold, then Cedar. Cedar kept digging his claws into Crystal's ears, but she tried to not pay attention to it. She needed to cross a stream.

"Augh!" Crystal yelped as she splashed into the cold water. At first, she could barely feel her legs, they were so numb with coldness. Finally when she was able to move, she took a step.

"NO!" The ground was so deep, she fell into the water, and only the pup's head could stick out from overhead.

Smoke wailed. "The water is too cold!"

All Crystal could think is, *I promised to keep them safe... I promised to keep them safe... don't let Poppy down... don't, don't, don't...*

"SWIM!" Crystal gurgled from under the water. "SWIM TO THE GROUND!" Cedar clamped his small jaws onto Smoke's scruff and helped his younger brother across, with Marigold closely behind them.

"Crystal! What about you?" Smoke yowled, his eyes glazed with tears. "I can make it!" She answered, waving her paws wildly as she paddled to the edge of the stream.

Cedar, Marigold, and even Smoke heaved Crystal out of the water, and she pushed herself up onto the grass. Her fur was flattened down from the freezing water, and she almost felt icicles hanging down from her nose.

"Oh, Crystal," Smoke said, burying his muzzle into her fur. "I'm sorry we left without you! I shouldn't of!" He wailed.

Crystal brushed her tail against his small poofy dark gray tail. "I'm okay, Smoke, I promise!" She said, slowly standing up.

"Should we keep going? Do you need to rest?" Marigold said nervously. Cedar looked a bit disappointed that there was a chance they were going to stop.

"We can keep going." Crystal said. "But first, prey."

"The grass is softer here!" Cedar squealed with a giggle. They had reached the field. Crystal had found a pile of rocks with a small, snug crevice in the middle.

"Can we sleep here?" Cedar asked. "May we!" Marigold yelled again. "You really need to work on that."

Crystal laughed. Watching pups annoy each other made her feel nostalgic. She remembered when she was small and used to fight with Tango and Stream.

"We can sleep here." Crystal said. Smoke ripped a piece of moss of the rock and placed it in the middle for a nice padding.

"Crystal?" Smoke whispered in the middle of the night. He was curled up next to her. "Mmm?" She murmured, her blue eyes half-open. "Why does the sky get dark at night?"

Crystal hesitated. She almost felt pressured by the little question, almost like Smoke would feel very disappointed and sad if she didn't answer, but Crystal didn't know the answer.

"Well," She whispered. "I'll answer it, and tell you a story." She felt Smoke's fur rise a bit with excitement. "Okay." He whispered back.

"Well, our leader, Echo, has a mother and father," She whispered. "And they have a mother and father, and they have a mother and father, and they have a mother and father. All the way in the beginning of time, there was the wolves that started everything; Day and Night. Night was a pitch-black wolf with beautiful, deep navy eyes, while Day was a sleek, white wolf with glittering yellow eyes like the sun." She tried to remember what Chestnut had told her when she was still small enough to sit on a maple leaf. "They lived in a world where the sky was all white. Both Day and Night didn't like this. They didn't like being the only color in a boring, white world. So they agreed to make the sky a light blue." She paused for a couple of seconds. "One day, Night told Day that he wanted a period of time to be his favorite color, black. Day thought this was only fair, and she agreed. So, half the day was black, and half was white. But soon, Day said that she wanted a little part in the period of time where the sky was black. She wanted to add yellow dots. She called these stars. Night said he wanted a part in the period of time where the sky was light blue. He made a big flaming ball he called the sun. After a while, Night and Day wanted to name their periods of time. They named them after themselves, night and day." Smoke let out a quick, high grunt of surprise. "Night and day!" He repeated. "Soon, they wanted more wolves. But they didn't know how to get them. So, at the time in between night and day, called sunset, they looked up at the sky, and simply asked for more wolves. Somebody far out in the galaxy must've heard, because the next day, thousands of happy wolves surrounded them. Night and Day were joyful to have a world of wolves." Crystal let out a tired laugh. "Little did they know, there was a whole big world of Gorilla hogs out there."

Smoke looked up at Crystal. "Thank you." He said, snuggling a little closer to her. "'Night." Smoke mumbled, falling asleep.

Crystal looked down at the pup. It made her feel old, even though *she* was a pup only a few weeks ago.

Chapter 29

"Crystal! Crystal!" Cedar repeated excitedly, pawing at Crystal's flank.

"Yes?" She finally answered, rolling her eyes. It was the early morning, and the wolves were walking through the giant field. There was a faint smell of dog, but it was old.

"This will be my tenth prey! The tenth prey I catch an' then eat! The tenth is obviously the most important, 'cause it's bigger than the first!" He squealed. "It's my ninth," Marigold said. "My fifth…" Smoke muttered, a little embarrassed he was so far behind.

Suddenly, there was a quick rustle through the bushes. It was a rabbit. The three pups bolted after it, Crystal following behind them.

"Wait, guys!" She shouted. "The rabbit's too fast! A-and, we're reaching Gorilla-hog territory…" But it was too late. A Gorilla-hog swooped up the three pups, and another came running to pick up her. She tried to bite, but the Gorilla hog just moved her to his other paw.

She ended up in a box. It had holes in the top, and was made of a weird brown material. At first she thought it was rocks or something, but it was oddly shaped and a bit squishy.

"Where are we?" Smoke said nervously. Crystal looked over, and in the corner of the box Marigold and Cedar were huddled together. Cedar looked more afraid than ever before; his brown fur was fluffed up. "My tenth prey," He whispered, his voice shaking.

Marigold sat up. "Okay, everyone, push the box to the side so the holes stick out. We can use our claws to break through it and escape. Then, we could find our way out and run away back home. Okay? Go!"

She rammed into the wall, knocking it over. Smoke squealed, and tumbled into the holey wall, making it rip. There was a gaping hole right where he had fell.

"It's open!" Cedar said, his fur flattening down with relief as he hopped through the hole. Marigold came after him, looking proud her idea worked. Then came Crystal.

Suddenly, a voice rasped, "Oh, forestdogs. My buddy's sister was a forest dog."

Crystal looked up to see a light gray dog with a white muzzle. "I'm Tommy," He said. The dog was old and raggedy. "Sadly, Mint passed away a month ago. Mm. Nice guy."

"I'm Crystal, this is Cedar, Marigold, Smoke… um, we gotta go, so, bye!" Crystal said frantically, picking up Cedar and Smoke by the scruff and hoisting Marigold onto her back.

"Goodbye." Tommy said, slowly turning around to walk into another room.

"This must be the door!" Crystal sighed with relief at the sight of the big light brown slab. The only other time she had been in a Gorilla Hog den was when she was a very, very small pup.

She pushed on it real hard, and luckily, it opened.

"M-may we go home after this?" Smoke asked nervously.

"Of course."

"Few."

"Tired out from all the excitement?"

"Well, if you can call it excitement."

"Heh."

"I'm really tired."

"Then sleep."

"I…" He yawned. "Am…"

Smoke was asleep. Crystal put him onto her back and walked out. They were next to the field, but not right next to it. Blocking it was a giant black streak that looked like it was made from individual black pebbles.

"What *is* that?" Marigold gawked, staring at the big black line. "I don't know, but we have to cross it." Crystal said, stepping up to pad across. Out of nowhere, a huge dark blue rock with Gorilla-hogs inside it flew past them.

"I don't wanna cross it!" Cedar whined. Marigold let out a small whimper of agreement.

"We have to." Crystal answered, struggling to keep her voice steady. Even she felt anxious about crossing the huge line.

She quickly ran to it, swerving to avoid a big rock that flew right behind her. She felt it's smooth surface fly past her. Marigold and Cedar screeched. Smoke woke up and squealed with them. Luckily, they made it safely to the other side. Or so Crystal thought.

"You're… t-t-t…" Marigold stuttered, her eyes huge. "TAIL!"

Suddenly, Crystal felt excruciating pain swipe through her body. She looked behind her to see the tip of her tail scratched and scraped up so much it looked as if it was going to fall off. Scarlet blood dripped out of the cuts, splattering the floor.

"It… must've been flattened by the rock…" She said, turning her head to lick off the blood. Marigold let out a loud whimper. "I'm okay, really," Crystal assured her.

"Okay…" She whispered, padding into the field swiftly with her head turned away so she couldn't see the blood.

"May we pleeease hunt?" Cedar asked hopefully when they finally reached the forest again.

Crystal nodded. "Okay, fine…" She said, rolling her eyes, but a grin plastered on her face.

She turned around to place Smoke, who was asleep again, on a patch of moss, laid a few leaves over him, and turned to start catching up with the pups.

"My tenth!" Cedar squealed after a while, picking up a little rat he had caught. "Yummy!" He crouched down and devoured the small critter.

"Someday, you'll be able to catch a full-grown fox," Crystal said with a laugh. "Or a deer."

"I'm gonna catch a deer now!" Marigold said, her ears perked up happily when she spotted a small speckled fawn nearby. Marigold bolted towards it, but when she was close to it, she crouched, not wanting to alarm it. Finally, Marigold pounced, scratching at biting at the deer's neck. She managed to kill it.

"My first deer! Well, the pups' first deer!" Marigold chirped, taking a bite out of it. Cedar stared at her for a few seconds, his eyes flashing with envy.

"I'm full and tired." Marigold said, letting out a small burp. Her and Crystal had shared the deer, and Cedar managed to catch a small mouse, and ate that along with the rat.

"I'll get Smoke and we can go back to camp," Crystal said, speed-walking away to get the fluffy gray pup.

When she saw Smoke, another dark grey wolf was next to him. At first, Crystal was about to let out an alarmed yowl, but then she realised who the wolf was.

Freeze.

Chapter 30

"Freeze?" Crystal muttered, stepping closer to see the wolf's eyes. They were the same icy blue as she remembered, but they had a sparkle in them.

"You're alive?! What?!" She shouted, almost falling from surprise. Freeze shook his head. "No." He said. His voice was still raspy, but it seemed a bit more clear. "All is we'll. You are good. Your pack is good. Danger is far, my dear; don't be afraid. One more warning, one more warning."

Crystal stepped back and blinked. Freeze was gone. She picked up Smoke and quickly padded away. *One more warning? What does that mean?*

"OH, you're all okay!" Poppy wailed in relief, gathering her pups around her and licking them all wildly. "Oh, little Smoke, how was it?" She asked kindly to her smallest pup. "Good!" Smoke said, looking content.

"GREAT!" Poppy gushed, giving him another few licks.

Echo stepped out. "The time has come." He said. Everyone looked out of their dens. Chestnut and Swift ran up to Crystal (who was hiding her tail) and gave her some licks, but then sat down and watched Echo.

"These pups," He said, waving his tail to Marigold and Cedar. "Are ready."

"Cedar, you have been a great hunter, a strong fighter, and seem to be always ready for anything.

Your eagerness to learn more has only made you less weak, and the time has come for you to stop training." Cedar almost squealed, but Poppy gave him a look so he wouldn't.

"Thank you, da- Echo!" He chirped happily, dipping his head and hopping off to the side next to Tango.

"Marigold." Echo said, looking at his daughter. The little white wolf stepped forward obediently.

"You have always been clever, and that really shows on your hunting abilities and fighting techniques. Even in the battles we could not win, I know you would somehow use your brain to make you better and stronger than the enemy. The time has come for you to stop training."

Marigold dipped he head, pressing her muzzle to his. "Thank you, Echo. I won't let you down, and although Cedar didn't say it, he won't let you down either." Cedar let out a small squee from the sides.

Echo walked back to his den, hoping he remembered all the words Rona had said to the pack whenever a pup was ready to quit training. He felt like a leader, a strong leader, even, and was happy he built up a pack.

"You did a great job." Poppy said, licking Echo's shoulder. She looked back at the empty bedding where the pups used to sleep. Now Smoke sat there alone, shivering constantly, obviously not sheltered enough to be comfortably warm.

"He needs to sleep with us." Echo said, picking up his son by the scruff and carrying him over to sit between Echo and Poppy.

"I'm afraid, Echo," Poppy whispered, looking down at her pup. "I'm afraid Smoke won't ever grow big or strong enough. He has barely grown since he was born."

Echo looked down at the pup. He was the right size for a pup, but not the right size for a pup about to stop training.

"He'll be okay. Just a bit more training." Echo said, briefly pressing his nose to his very dark gray fur. It almost looked like the night sky.

"Echo…" Willow asked, padding up to the big gray wolf. It was a windy autumn afternoon. "I feel like I haven't done much for the past few days. I feel unwanted."

"You aren't unwanted! Just, a lot of stuff has happened, and…" Echo trailed off.

"I understand. I guess I just want something cool to happen to me. Everyday has sort of been… almost the same."

"I bet something will happen that's exciting. It always does." Echo responded, padding to get a piece of prey, and putting it in front of Willow.

"I'll hunt myself." He said, glaring down at the prey. "But thanks anyway."

"*Sigh*…" Willow sat down on a patch of moss, looking up at the sky. He had never really believed in all the stories his father told him, but today he was desperate.

"Dad?" He asked, staring. It was almost night. The sky was a mix of purple and orange, and the sun was too low for Willow to see through the trees.

"I need to ask you… is this really my destiny? To be in a pack? To feel *invisible* in a pack? I… don't want to be selfish. I'm a beta. But… still… I don't know. I don't even know if everyone likes me."

The wind spiraled leaves around him, almost like he was the center of a tornado.

'Shhhh,' the wind muffled, almost sounding like a real wolf voice. "Shhhon…" it seemed to say. "Shhhon?" Willow repeated. "Shone? Sun? Son?"

"Son!" He chirped, but then shook his head quickly and looked down, realising he probably sounded like a pup.

"Yes…" The wind answered him. It sounded more clear now, more like his father's voice.

"Willow, this isn't your destiny, but your destiny is to stay in this pack. But if you want something to happen, if you want to not feel invisible, then… do something. Make something. Help someone. I will be watching."

The voice stopped and the leaves fell slowly to the ground. The wind was all gone.

"Echo, I…" Willow paused, reconsidering. "I'm gonna go find a mate. I need one." Echo's tail fluffed up from being so surprised. "A mate? But…

you never…" "I need to. I need to do things for the pack."

"But a mate? You can do other things to help our pack!" Echo protested. "You've never wanted a mate, Willow. I don't want you to do something you don't want to do just for our pack."

"I want to do it for our pack!" Willow spat back at him, but then stepped back, looking embarrassed. "Sorry. I might not even let *her* be in the pack… just the pups."

"But what if all the pups die?" Echo asked nervously.

There was silence.

"Goodbye, Echo," Willow said, padding away. "I'll be back… sometime. With pups." He forced himself to take the few small steps out of camp. Everyone was yelling, "Goodbye! Goodbye! We'll miss you!"

"Alright, Willow," Willow said to himself, almost in an angry tone. "You're going to find a mate!"

Chapter 30

"I don't want to." Willow panted, falling onto the ground, exhausted. "I don't want a mate. I want pups. Pups that could grow up in our pack from the beginning. Pups that I own."

He had been travelling for weeks now, and he was in a very odd place; there was giant rock towers everywhere, so high he couldn't see the top. Big blue, red, black, and white rocks zoomed passed him a lot. There was always one next to him. No wolves were there, only dogs and cats and pigeons.

"There's bound to be some stray pups living around here…" Willow said, still a scrap of determination inside of him, forcing him to go on.

"You! The big baby!" A tough deep voice yelled. A giant black and dark brown dog with huge claws and teeth padded up to him.

"What're you doin' here? You're a little pea!" *pea?* Willow thought. *What's a pea? That's probably bad.*

"Actually," Willow said, trying to sound confident. "You're the pea!"

"Me? A pea? Are you insane?!" The giant dog shouted, stomping his big paw down on Willow's tail when he turned around.

"NOBODY CALLS ROCK A PEA!" The dog yelled, quickly lowering his head to bite Willow's neck. He swerved, avoiding the dog's giant jaws, and wriggled out from under the dog. Willow jumped on his back, and then crouched down to bite his tail. The dog squealed, and flung his head down, sending Willow slipping down his back and landing right in front of him. He ran as fast as he could.

There was a fence straight in front of him. It looked like it was made out of something skinny and shiny.

Willow managed to slide through a hole in the fence, but the giant dog was too big. He snarled and spat as Willow sat in front of him on the other side, looking smug.

"So, your name was Rock?" Willow said. The dog barked angrily, but it sounded more like a roar.

"You know any stray pups around here?" He asked, and Rock growled loudly. "You think I'm gonna tell a dumb pipsqueak like you?"

"If I'm dumb then why did I just outsmart you?" Willow said. Rock paused, and then roared again.

"If I see you past this fence, I will bite your head off, no questions asked!" He announced, and padded away, his paws making a loud *thump* on the ground with every step.

Willow turned around. He was in a yard of some sorts, but the grass was all dead and brown-ish and weeds grew everywhere.

"SCRAM!" A gorilla-hog voice snorted, and a scrawny old lady with a big stick that was curved into a handle at the top limped out of the door of the den next to the yard. Willow ran out under the fence again, running swiftly in the other direction than Rock.

Willow sniffed the air. Folded in between all the disgusted fumes was a sweet, honey scent. *Pups!* He thought, joy flowing through him like a wave in a stream.

"Hi, puppie- Oh no." A mother was with them! And worst of all, they weren't puppies... they were kittens.

"Stay away from my kittens!" The mother hissed, waving her long tail wildly. She waved her claw at him, and Willow stepped away. "Sorry!"

I'm gonna need food sometime soon... Willow thought. It wasn't morning anymore, it was late in the evening, already after sunset, so it was pitch black. The strange town was much creepier in the dark.

Instead of searching for pups, he searched for food now. Tomorrow he would search for pups. Luckily, he smelled another animal- a dog. It was young, about the same age as Crystal or Tango.

"Hello?" Willow said, looking into an alley between two rock towers. The small dog was curled up, eating a pigeon. "Hm?" She said, turning around.

"Hi. I'm Willow." Willow said, keeping his distance just in case the dog was violent.

"I'm Lila!" She chirped, examining him.

"Oh you poor thing! You're so skinny and weak!" Lila talked to him like he was a helpless pup.

"I'm fine. Just a little hungry." Willow said, narrowing his eyes a bit with anger. He didn't like it when wolves or dogs treated him like that.

"Here! Have some!" She said, pushing another pigeon towards him. Willow crouched down and took a quick couple of bites, and then started to walk away.

"No, sleep here! I insist! You look so tired!" Lila squealed, waving her tail, almost like she was beckoning Willow. He rolled his eyes, but he was thankful that this dog wasn't constantly threatening him.

Lila talked all night. Willow found it a bit amusing, considering she thought he looked awfully tired.

"I have to go," Willow said in the morning quickly, and ran off before Lila could even say goodbye to him.

Pups. Pups. Dog pups. Or even better, wolf pups. But we won't find them here. Willow sniffed the air, over and over, trying to find at least the smallest scent of pup. Finally, he picked up the scent.

"Puppies!" Willow chirped. Two very small pups were sitting asleep in a square brown hollow thing. He stepped back, examining them. The pups looked exactly like Rock! What if they would attack him once they get older? *No, no, if they grow up in our pack, they'll like us,* Willow thought. *And they'd be as big and strong as rock!*

He turned around, racing back to the edge of the strange rock tower town, so he could find his way back home. But that's when it started to snow. Hard.

The pups squealed. They seemed excited that they got to experience their first snowfall, but one was shivering so wildly that Willow almost dropped it.

"Are you okay?" Willow asked the pup in the kindest voice he could do. The pup squealed. "I need to get some shelter…"

He looked around, trying to find even a scrap of anything that would be warm or furry, other than dog and cat hairs all over.

A cup! He put the puppy in the cup, and then carried it in his jaws, along with the other stronger pup. He knew what a cup was because once when he was as small as the pup he was holding, his father found a cup and bit a hole in it, making it look like a tunnel, and then used it to make a squirrel trap. Whenever the squirrels jumped inside, he would quickly kill them. It got him three free squirrels. His father was always smart like that.

The pup was still trembling. He tried to lick it to make it warm, but it wasn't working. The pup was gone.

Willow laid it down on the ground. He felt horrible leaving a dead pup just sitting on the ground, but the rock was too strong for him to dig through it.

This one needs to live... He thought, carrying the other pup, hoping it was strong enough to live.

"GASP!" He had been travelling forever, and Willow and the pup finally got back to a forest-y place! He didn't recognise it, though. He looked down off the edge, and a giant streak of black was in front of him. THE ROAD. Another thing his father had told him about.

"We'll have to cross it." He told the pup. It squealed in terror, or excitement. Willow couldn't tell.

He padded across it, and luckily, it was surprisingly empty. At one point a rock flew past him, but only once. He was in the forest.

Chapter 31

"Willow! You're back!" Echo chirped, sounding like a puppy, but not really minding because he was so happy.

"A pup?!" He shouted, looking down at the pup in Willow's jaws. "He will join our pack, and grow up to be strong and mighty. I'll take care of him… feed him, train him, everything." Willow said, looking down at the small black and brown pup.

"Willow, this is really nice of you. I… can't believe you went through all the trouble of finding a pup, just for our pack!" Echo said, licking his friend's shoulder.

"He needs a name!" Chestnut said. "What do you think, Willow?"

Willow thought for a while. Even if Rock was rude, Willow still felt a bit bad for stealing what seemed to be his son. His name should be related to Rock.

"Maybe Boulder," Willow thought. "I think he'll grow up big and strong, and boulders are big and heavy." The pup let out a little high pitched grunt.

"He likes it!" Tango said, putting his paw in front of the pup. Boulder put his little paw onto Tango's. Even though Tango was still a young wolf, he looked giant compares to the tiny scrap.

It only took a few days for the pup to be as big as Cedar, even though it was still only 2 or 3 weeks old. he learned quickly, and Willow even taught him some fighting moves.

"Cedar!" Boulder said, bouncing up to the little brown wolf. "Teach me some fighting moves! Pah! Pah!" He waved his claws in the air. "Fine!" Cedar said, padding in front of him.

"Crystal said this was the most effective." He said proudly. "I mastered it!" "How do you do it?" Boulder asked, his eyes shining.

"You slide under your enemy, and then slash it's stomach when you're under them! And then, they die!"

Boulder copied what Cedar did all the time, which made Willow a bit worried he was going to turn out like the small wolf, super energetic and sometimes disrespectful, but Boulder was surprisingly still the nice, excited to learn puppy he was.

"Willow?" Boulder asked once he was about 2 months old. "Could I start training now?" Willow thought for a moment. He didn't want to train this puppy too young, but he seemed eager.

"Sure." Willow said, waving his bushy tail. Boulder squealed in happiness. "Let's do it now!" "Hold on, I need to tell Echo," Willow said, padding up to Echo, who had just came back from hunting with Swift and Tango.

"Echo, I was thinking Boulder could start his training with me," Willow said. Echo nodded. "Sure."

"Good news, Bo-" Willow started to say, but Boulder was gone. First, Willow wasn't nervous at all; he might have just gone to eat a piece of prey, or go to get something from the den.

"Hey, Grayson," Willow said, padding up to the gray-brown wolf. "Is Boulder sick or something?" Grayson shrugged. "Haven't smelled him."

"Boulder? Where are you?" Willow shouted. "He went to hunt with Cedar, I think." Skyler said, carrying a bit of deer in her jaws.

"Cedar isn't very reliable..." Willow muttered, racing into the forest, trying to find the scent of Cedar or Boulder. It was like looking for the pups all over again.

Finally, he picked up a scent. "Cedar! Boulder!" Willow yelled as he followed the scent. It stopped abruptly at a rock and Willow couldn't smell it anymore. "What did they do, roll in deer poop?" He murmured under his breather.

"Oh- uh, hey, Willow..." It was Cedar, stalking low against the ground like he didn't want to be seen. Willow turned his head to look at the brown wolf, but he lunged into a nearby bush before he could see him.

"What are you hiding?" Willow asked, raising his eyebrow. "Uh... nothing..."

"We fell in the mud."

This voice was Boulder's. The brown-black puppy padded up from behind the tree, his coat drenched in the awful light brown muck, which completely hid his usual scent.

"Why does your smell stop at this *rock*, then?" Willow said.

"Because Cedar climbed on it and jumped off, and then I followed him. We tumbled all the way down to a mud pool." Boulder replied. He talked surprisingly seriously, however, his eyes glimmered with amusement, making it look like he was trying not to laugh.

"It's not funny!" Cedar squealed, who must've seen Boulder's eyes. The puppy started squeaking with laughter.

"Let's get you back to the dens," Willow said, rolling his eyes. Boulder, who was still mud-drenched, followed him, but Cedar stayed still in the bush.

"Cedar?"

"There's no way I'm going back to camp!"

"Why?"

"I'd be so embarrassed!"

"That's the price to pay for jumping in the mud!"

The small wolf groaned, and stepped out of the shrub. His whole body was covered in mud, even more than Boulder's.

"What happened here?" Echo asked, quickly walking up to the animals.

"They fell in the mud!" Willow replied, curling his lips in a bit to prevent him from laughing his fur off.

"Shut up!" Cedar shouted, kicking Willow in the thigh.

"Show respect to the Beta, Cedar," Echo said. The small brown wolf looked more outraged than ever.

"I should be the Beta! I'm your son! You just said this Hog-head was your son because you just wanted him to be Beta! You thought he was better than me! You STILL do!" Cedar screamed, running away in the direction of the cliff where he used to be trained.

Echo sighed. "Sorry about Cedar. He's still… well, rude, even after his ceremony." Willow shrugged. "I'll take Boulder to the stream to get him cleaned up." Willow said, nudging the pup next to him.

"The stream? Didn't you say you almost drowned there?" Boulder asked, looking pretty nervous, despite him always being eager and brave.

"I won't dunk you in, Boulder," Willow said, smirking. "I'm just going to pick some up with some moss or something and then rub it on you to get the mud off." "gross…" Boulder muttered.

"What's wrong now?" Willow asked. "The specks of moss will get all over me!" Willow smirked again. "You'll live."

Chapter 32

"That one seems more effective than the last to me." Boulder said. They were practicing hunting techniques. The pup still hadn't been able to catch his first prey yet, but he was getting pretty close.

"Yeah…" Willow agreed, swiping the dust-covered dead rabbit that they were using to practise.

"May we try these out now?" Boulder asked eagerly, looking as hopeful as ever.

"I suppose…" Willow said. The puppy squealed. "Wait," Willow demanded. "On one condition. Promise me that you will give it to Echo, and not eat it for yourself?"

Boulder hesitated. It was obvious he wanted to eat his first catch.

"Without Echo, you would still be a stray on the streets of the town of rock towers. You would've frozen to death. And I would be dead, too. I would've drowned."

The puppy's eyes grew wide; Willow didn't know if it was because of fear or gratitude towards the Alpha. He quickly nodded.

"Now let's go!" Willow said, softly hitting Boulder with his tail to hurry him up.

"Yay!" He squealed, back to his normal, bubbly self.

"Prey isn't running well…" Boulder panted. They had been walking forever, and they could barely find a fur of any prey.

Winter had been growing cold, and it had snowed more, leaving icicles hanging off of every branch and slanted rock. A thick, white blanket was spread around the whole ground.

Blanket... Willow thought. His father had taught him so much Gorilla-hog words he was getting a bit nervous. What if his father used to live with them?

Willow had never really liked animals that lived with the Gorilla-hogs, even though half his pack WAS them.

"Mouse!" Boulder squealed, interrupting Willow's thoughts. "Really?" He asked, pushing through the snow to reach the little pup.

Boulder crouched down in hunting position, carefully pressing his paws on the snow. He was so light, he could stand on top of the snow without falling through. *That must make it much easier,* Willow thought.

The mouse was right in front of him, digging downwards through the snow, probably looking for any little morsels of food.

It was perfect. A perfect crouch, the perfect position, the perfect length; just one jump and Boulder would be on top of the poor little mouse, and there would be finally a bit of prey for the pack.

CCCRaaaCK... "What?" Boulder yelped. He fell through the snow, alerting the mouse, and making him scurry away.

"So much for first prey!" Willow spat, but
Boulder was barrelling after the mouse.
"BOULDER! STOP, IT'S OKAY!" the pup just
kept running.

"I got it!" Willow heard Boulder's voice yelp
happily. He padded up with the mouse in his jaws.

"Woah. You're quick, Boulder! As quick as Swift,
and his name is Swift!" Willow said with delight,
astonished by the pup's speed. He puffed up his
chest with pride. "Thank you!"

"Wanna go back to camp, or try for more?"
Willow asked, noticing the pup's eyes drooping.
"More! More!" He yelped, desperately trying to
open his eyes all the way.

"Let's try more tomorrow," Willow said. The pup
murmured something and then let his eyes close. He
was asleep.

Willow smirked, picking up Boulder the scruff
and carrying him and the prey back to the dens.

"Any goodies?" Poppy asked, padding out of her
den. "Just one peice of prey caught by Boulder."
Willow answered. "Ah! Congratul-" But then she
noticed that Boulder asleep. "First prey to exciting,
ey?" She said, looking up at Willow. he nodded.

"Here, Echo," Willow said, padding up to Echo
with the mouse. "Boulder caught this, and was
going to give it to you, but he fell asleep.

"Thank you, Willow, but I don't need it. Give it to
the pack." Echo said, pushing the mouse back

towards him. *What a great leader. Maybe someday I'll be a leader.*

"Hello, there, Boulder." A voice said. It was strange; everything was foggy and a bit blue-ish, almost giving a paranormal look to the forest. Nothing looked normal.

"Hi!" Boulder chirped, scanning the area for some sort of creature that was talking to him. "Where are you?"

"It's me, Rock," The voice said. "Crystal, the one in your pack… she got a message from her friend. One more warning, I think it was, but I don't remember. Freeze couldn't deliver the warning, but I can. So-" Boulder yowled. "Does this mean you're dead? You're my dada, right?"

"The cold was too much." Rock answered, dipping his head like he was saying hello.

"It's almost time for the storm." He said. "A storm? Like… snowstorm?" Boulder asked, tipping his head.

"Rona." Rock said. "Echo's sister. It will be the storm of her." Then he disappeared into fog.

"Boulder?" Willow prodded the pup awake. "You've been sleeping for a long time! I thought you were going to sleep through winter!" He laughed.

"Something's gonna happen! Rock told me!" Boulder yelled, wriggling out from under Willow's paw. "Rock? You mean…" Willow started, but trailed off.

"Crystal!" Boulder screamed, jumping on top of the gray wolf. "What?!" She asked loudly, pushing him off.

"Freeze- I don't know who that is, but Freeze- w-warning, storm… storm of.. Uh…" Echo ran up to them. "The storm of Rona. My parents told me in a dream."

"Rona?" Crystal repeated, her eyes sparkling with a mixture of nervousness and excitement. *I know I shouldn't be happy about this, but it will be one of my first battles!*

"My sister. We need to find her!" Echo yelled, nudging Crystal out of bed. "We need to find the rest of the pack and tell them."

Echo quickly ran out, gathering the pack and telling them the mission they had to go on.

"Will we be going just with Echo?" Boulder asked Crystal. "I assume so," She answered. Boulder smiled a bit. *An adventure!*

Chapter 33

"This isn't something to smile about, Boulder. We could be in great danger." Echo said. Boulder had barely noticed he had been smiling almost the whole time.

"I'm sorry, Echo. But I'm just excited for my first mission!" Boulder protested. But Echo looked kindly at him. "It's okay. I have to admit- I'm a little excited to show Rona how far I've gotten in life. Now I'm an Alpha and she's the one that isn't respected; wandering through the forest!"

"Maybe we should climb down the cliff. I assume Rona would be looking for prey down there, since there is much more land and we didn't catch it already." Crystal suggested.

"Okay. You can climb down yourself, I'll carry Boulder." Echo responded, leading them to the training cliff.

"Do we just jump down?" Crystal asked, struggling to keep her voice steady as she looked at the dizzining drop.

"We climb down. The hill isn't completely down, just at an extreme angle." Echo said, crouching down to pick up Boulder.

Echo started to inch his way down with Boulder hanging in his jaws, but Crystal hesitated. She had looked down this drop before while training- or saving a pup from falling- but she never tried to climb down it.

"It's okay, Crystal, If you fall I'll catch you,"
Echo said, surprisingly calm for trying to slide down
a giant cliff.

"O-okay." She said, and made the mistake of
jumping out a bit instead of turning around and just
climbing down.

Crystal barrelled downwards, screeching her heart
out. She was going to die! There was no way she
would survive… no way…

CCC…. "I'm alive?" Crystal said. She was
hanging on a root sticking out of the cliff, which
was about to break. She twisted and unsheathed her
claws, letting them hang onto the edge of the cliff.

"You're almost to the bottom!" Echo shouted to
her. Boulder nodded, and pointed his paw down.
"Look how close you are!"

Crystal looked down. Only about three normal-
sized tree lengths down was the ground!

She tried to climb down quickly now; she was
eager to get to bottom.

Crystal looked up. She was now on the ground,
waiting on the ground for her friends, who were as
close as she was a few minutes ago. Luckily, they
reached the ground safely.

"Now we look for Rona," Echo announced,
placing Boulder back on the ground. "Let's hunt
first!" Boulder said, bouncing into the forest.

The forest floor wasn't covered in as much snow
as before, just a thin sheet of it. Every time Crystal

stepped, she would feel her paw reach the wet, muddy ground.

"Echo! Lemme show you my hunting skills!" Boulder yapped, sniffing the air. "I smell a trace of a fawn!"

"Very good," Echo said, dipping his head. "You seem to have been doing great in your lessons with Willow. At this age, other pups would barely know how to properly crouch.

Boulder puffed up his chest proudly, and ran into the forest.

"I'll hunt a bit too," Crystal said, padding in a different direction. Echo nodded, and settled down on the grass.

"Fawn fawn fawn faaawn!" Boulder sung under his breath as he followed the scent. Finally, he saw the small deer, looking lost for their mother.

Boulder crouched, slowly stalking near the fawn. It's grassy scent weaved around him.

The fawn turned around. *Dang it.* Boulder thought. *It noticed me!*

But strangely, instead of running off, the fawn examinined Boulder. He was frozen with shock. "I... I..." Boulder stuttered.

"I speak dog and wolf." the fawn said, surprising Boulder even more. "My name is Meadow. Lots of wolves have tried to kill me before, but I like to shock them instead. You look like a dog, but you smell like wolf. You were raised by them, yes?" The fawn had a nice accent, one that almost calmed Boulder.

"I'm Boulder. Could I… please kill you? My pack is hungry." Boulder asked.

"No." Meadow said. "Instead, have some of my prey," She said, pushing three rats towards him.

Boulder was about to deny them, and say he could do it for himself, but he was too hungry to.

"Thanks," Boulder said, picking up the rats. "I thought fawns just ate berries, though?" Meadow nodded. "I just have these for passer-byers. There's a lot." Boulder nodded, and then quickly ran away.

"Three ra-ats! Three ra-ats!" Boulder shouted with joy as he frolicked back to Echo. Crystal was there, too, carrying a small mouse the size of a leaf.

"You found THREE rats?!" Crystal gasped, dropping her tiny mouse. "Three rats!" Boulder repeated, trying to sound like he was proud of himself.

"That's… incredible!" Echo said, padding up to Boulder, who was trying so hard not to burst out the truth that he was trembling. Echo and Crystal were proud of him- why tell them the truth?

"Yep… I caught three rats!" Boulder lied. "Anyway, let's eat and then be on our way."

The wolves and dog ate. The food made Crystal feel stronger than ever before. She felt like she could run miles.

"A field!" Crystal chirped once they reached a big open area with tall grass sprouting everywhere. "I thought the only nearby field was the one near the black streak," She said.

"A wolf!" Boulder yowled, waving his paw towards a dark figure crouched down in the tall grass.

"Who are you?" Echo said, padding up to the raggedy wolf. He rose up, one of his eyes completely white, the other a gray-ish color. He was even older than Freeze.

The wolf wailed. "THE BLUE-EYED GRAY CLOUD!" He yelled.

Boulder looked at Echo, and then Crystal. They were both gray and blue eyed. "I don't think it is us." Echo said. "It must be Rona."

"Where did you see them?" Crystal said softly, not trying to alarm the old fleabag.

"In the... the... corn... sh-sharp... aughh..." The wolf died right in front of them, which would've traumatized the life out of Boulder, but he was too determined to focus on stuff like that.

"Sharp corn? What could that mean?" Crystal thought, wrapping her tail around her paws, almost like she was cold.

Chapter 34

"Maybe he means rough corn." Boulder said. "Yeah!" Echo agreed quickly. "Corn leaves are pretty rough. Maybe she's out in some sort of corn field."

"Obviously we can't ask the wolf for more help," Crystal said, flicking her tail towards the lifeless body next to them.

"Let's sleep first. I don't want you guys to be too tired while we travel." Echo said, eying Boulder, who was so happy about the mission he barely noticed that he was about to collapse with drowsiness.

"Okay…" Boulder said, lying down on the tall grass. The moment he closed his eyes, Boulder instantly fell asleep.

"Corn," Crystal said. They were walking through the field the next morning, looking around for even the smallest kernel of corn.

"I think that's some over there!" Boulder chirped, bouncing over to a patch of tall grass.

"Nope, just more darn grass!" He spat, letting his claws come out and slashing the grass, sending little pieces of it falling to the ground.

"What is that?" Crystal asked, tipping her head to the left. She squinted her eyes, and far, far away, was a strange looking fence of some sorts made of skinny silver strings.

"Barbed wire fence." Echo said. "When I was young, one of those wire fences was right behind my mother's bed, and since I slept with her, I was constantly wandering off to see the fence. My mother told me to stay away, because some parts stick out and scratch you, or even get stuck under your skin and that could make you really sick. We should steer clear of it."

"Corn might be behind it!" Crystal chirped, disobeying Echo and running towards it. Boulder followed, and then with a sigh, Echo did too.

Before he knew it, Echo and the others were sitting in front of the fence, peering through the spaces in it.

"Dare you to paw at it!" Boulder challenged Crystal.

"I decline. Echo said it was dangerous, and I won't disobey him."

Even though you just did, Echo thought, but he didn't even care that much. He still wasn't that used to being looked up to and obeyed, even after all the months he had been Alpha.

"Thanks," Echo said to Crystal. "Anyway we need to find this corn. Rona has to be somewhere near it."

"Echo, I think there's corn over there. I'm being serious." Boulder murmured, his eyes widening as he looked into the distance.

"CORN!" Crystal yowled, overjoyed. "Can we go over, Echo?" She asked, sensing the gentle wolf acknowledged her not obeying him last time.

"Yeah! I'll come too, actually!" Echo said, running swiftly ahead to see the corn.

"It's corn!" He announced. "Now, we need to get serious and find Rona."

Crystal and Boulder agreed.

After awhile of searching through the corn, it started to rain, wiping out the scent of Rona they were following.

Luckily, right away they saw the wolf's bushy gray tail swishing through some corn.

"RONA!" Echo growled, lunging onto the tail. Crystal and Boulder ran up, pulling the wolf around. "Hey! Watch it!" A raspy voice yelled at them. "And I'm *not* Rona!"

"Oh. Sorry. You can go on your way." Boulder said, backing away, but Crystal scooted him back with her tail.

The wolf swung her head around. Her paws, underbelly, chest, and muzzle were light gray, and one of her eyes were lime and the other dark cactus green, differentiating her from Rona.

"Have you seen an all-gray blue-eyed female wolf around here?" Echo asked her, trying to sound as kind as possible just in case she was hot-tempered.

"I'm seeing her!" She said, glaring at Crystal, and then whipping her head back to Echo. "Let go of me and leave me alone, creeps!" She shouted, stomping away.

"She seemed so nice." Crystal joked, but Boulder didn't hear. He was already running after the wolf.

"Be serious. Are you sure you really didn't see any wolf that looks like that?" He sounded as stern and serious as ever, nothing like how Boulder's bubbly voice had ever sounded.

"FIIINE. I did see some idiot shuffling her way under that wire fence and running into the stumpfarm." The wolf responded, rolling her eyes.

"Stumpfarm?" Boulder asked.

"Yeah, the place with all the tree stumps behind the fence. It used to be a wonderful forest... my home... but then some dumb old Gorilla-hogs came in with their claws-on-sticks and cut 'em down. Why am I even telling you this? I hate you!" She yelled, running away quickly so Boulder couldn't catch up.

Everyone looked at each other, all thinking the same thing. *How do we get under it?*

"We could dig under it." Echo said, pawing at the ground quickly, making some grass and dirt spray out behind him.

For the next half hour or so, they dug and dug and dug. But, when they were about halfway, they were too close under the fence, so the roof of the tunnel had some of the wires sticking out.

Crystal and Boulder, being smaller than Echo, could press their stomachs against the ground and slide under, but every time Echo tried it scratched him, leaving the fur on his back haggard and the skin under it scraped and bloody.

"Do we keep digging the same tunnel?" Crystal asked. "I'll be pretty tired if we have to dig a new one."

"Keep digging this one!" Echo insisted. "I'll find a way to get under without shredding my fur and skin."

So, they did, and finished a bit later. Crystal and Boulder slipped under first, leaving Echo stuck behind them.

Echo couldn't help to yowl once he slid under. "Are you okay?!" Crystal urgently asked onced Echo came out the other side. "Y-yeah, I think," He responded, but... he wasn't.

"The fur is so, so ripped up, and his skin has so much scratches! Once all the blood dries, it'll be super hard to get it out of the fur!" Crystal said, inspecting Echo's back. Boulder let out a sad whimper.

"So, I can lick it up right when it stops," Echo said, continuing to walk. Crystal let out a sad sigh, and agreed, following him.

Chapter 35

"A hole?"

The wolves and dog were gathered around a hole deep into the ground, which looked like an abandoned den for a fox. Slush(After it raining, the ground was covered in slush instead of snow) was sliding into it, probably the cause of what made the fox leave.

"It smells strange, but like a wolf," Boulder said. "What if Rona is hiding in there?"

"I'll go first," Echo said, carefully stepping in. "Rona?" He asked nervously as he padded in.

"What? Who are you?"

It was Rona. Rona's voice.

"It's Echo, and we will not let you lead a storm!"

"How did you get here?" She growled, slashing her paw against the scar that was already on Echo's face.

"We won't let you make our pack break apart. We need to kill you now!" Echo told her, which at first Boulder thought wasn't smart at all, but when he walked in, he realised the wolf looked very skinny, sick, and raggedy. She wouldn't be strong enough to even bite.

"First, my son betrays me, then my mate wanders off and DIES, and now this? I die? No. I don't die!"

"Wha-" Echo started to say, but was pushed away by Rona, who shot out of the hole, under the fence, through the corn, and disappeared into the tall grass.

"She's going to our dens!" Echo yelled. "We need to go. Now!"

They all ran after Rona, and for the first time, Echo didn't feel a thing as he slid under the fence. He was too pumped with worry and adrenaline.

"Echo..." Boulder panted after a long hour of running. "It's the middle of the night, and I'm really tired. Rona is much weaker than us. She's probably behind us, or sleeping."

"I suppose it's late. I guess we can sleep." Echo responded, a trace of worry in his voice.

The others had fell asleep instantly, but Echo was still too nervous to fall asleep. What if his entire pack died, or was heavily wounded? Rona might have been weak, but there's a chance she is still strong enough to kill. She was always the strongest pup, then the strongest wolf, then the strongest leader. Even Barn, who was trying super hard to catch up, couldn't even outshine Rona.

Finally, sleep found Echo, but it was a light sleep, and almost every half hour he would wake up, trembling with anxiety.

"Echo..." It was his mother alone. Immediately Echo knew this was another dream, perhaps a good one, but he still prepared for the worst.

"Hello, mother..." Echo said, looking at his paws, which were shiny and blue from the light his mother was giving off. All the spirits that had appeared in Echo's dreams were blue, translucent, and glowing.

"What is wrong, child?" She asked, padding slightly closer to Echo.

"I'm afraid for my pack. What if they get hurt? Is there really going to be a *storm of Rona?*" Echo asked nervously, shuffling his paws. His mother gave him a long hard stare.

"One will be wounded, three will be mildly hurt." She started.

"Who'll be wounded? Will they surv-"

"Let me finish."

"O-okay."

"The wolf with mighty power will be left in the dirt."

"Am I the wolf of mighty power?"

"Goodbye, Echo."

"Wait! No!" Echo begged, but his mother already had faded away into the fog, which was being slowly washed away by sunlight shining bright through the trees.

"We need to go now!" Echo said, prodding the others awake. Boulder smacked his lips and stood up. "Should we catch some prey?" He asked. *Meadow must be around here...*

"No time!" Echo responded, barrelling in the direction of the cliff.

"D-do we climb?" Crystal asked, looking up to it. She could barely see the top, but she could smell a little bit of her pack's familiar scent.

"There's a bunch of rocks jutting out. We could climb those." Echo said, crouching down to pick up Boulder, who swerved and avoided his jaws.

"I think I want to climb it up on my own. May I?" He asked, his brown eyes wide with hope.

"I suppose. But you go first so if you fall I catch you." Echo responded. Boulder let out a yelp of happiness and sprung up on the cliff, using his little claws to inch his way up.

"This is fun!" Boulder finally squeaked after a long time of silence as the other wolves climbed up the cliff. He bounced off the jutted out rock he was standing on to scramble onto another.

"This is… strange." Crystal said, trembling with fear as she dared to look under her, but too proud to admit it.

"Wow, Boulder, you're almost at the top!" Echo said, sensing Crystal's fears and trying to change the subject. The pup let out a quick yowl of joy as he sprung up to the top of the cliff, where the ground was flat.

Echo soon came up behind him, delighted to have his paws on another flat surface.

"C'mon, Crystal!" Boulder insisted, beckoning the struggling young wolf. "I'm coming!" She answered, and spat in fury as a sharp rock sticking out of the cliff scraped her pads.

Finally, Crystal reached the top, her paws aching and arms stiff.

"Now let's go." Echo demanded, quickly turning around to run into the familiar forest.

Crystal began to hear noises of fighting; growling, roaring, slashing, yowling. She became tense. *Surely the pack can fight Rona. I mean, she's scrawny and weak. ...right?*

When the three reached the dens, the fight with Rona was in full action.

Chapter 36

"Get off him!" Echo yowled as he lunged onto Rona, who was on top of Grayson, about to bite his neck. After Echo knocked her off, Grayson stumbled away, Skyler quickly running up to him to guide him away.

A growl rumbled in Boulder's throat as he jumped onto Rona, who was already trying her hardest to fight Echo.

With a loud screech, Rona flung both of them off her, and ran up to slash Boulder on his belly. He screamed, blood gushing from the huge scratch.

"Boulder!" Willow shouted as he picked up his son, carrying him quickly to the big den. "Are you okay?"

"I'm okay!" Boulder said, jumping out of the grassy bed, adrenaline still pumping throughout him, refusing to make the cut hurt.

"Okay, but don't jump on her again! Just give her a few leg nips!" Willow said, running out to help his friends. Boulder padded unsteadily behind him.

"Echo…" Rona said, her eyes opening slightly as she looked at her brother. "You have a pack now. Mmm."

"See how far I've gotten?" Echo snarled. "Hard to believe I used to sit around all day, huh?"

"You still look like the same fat blob you did back then!" Rona smirked, waving her tail.

Someone started growling loudly in the crowd. Boulder turned around to see who, and it was Poppy.

"No one calls my mate a fat blob!" She shouted, lunging herself at Rona, who let out a quick yelp. Poppy was surprisingly an amazing fighter; she got in a lot of scratches, bites, scrapes. But... Rona did too.

Poppy screeched as Rona bit her leg hard. It had a huge in it, and blood seeped out, splattering the ground with scarlet drops.

"Mom!" Cedar yelled, running over to Poppy, licking her wound wildly. "Are you okay? Are you okay?" She nodded feebly, slowly getting up, her injured leg pressed against her stomach so she wouldn't step on it.

The whole pack stared in horror. "Anybody else want to try to fight me?" Rona spat, letting her claws slide out a little more.

"You hurt my mom..." Cedar growled. "Now we hurt you!" Marigold finished, padding up beside her brother. Storm walked up too, unsheathing his claws.

All three wolves lunged at Rona, who struggled under the weight of them all. She waved her paw, sending Cedar skidding across the dirty floor.

He ran back up, continuing to fight, despite the giant scratch on his back. Finally, Rona managed to get them all off herself.

"I'm not gonna leave this place without one of you dead!" She announced, glancing around the crowd. "I'd like to see you try." Crystal muttered.

"Hmm?" Rona asked.

"I said…" Crystal started, her voice raising. "I'd like to see you try!"

She barrelled towards Rona, but she dodged, sending Crystal face-first into the ground. "Enough." Rona said, crouching down to bite Crystal's neck. She struggled to get up, but Rona pushed her back down onto the ground.

"Crystal! No!" Storm yowled as Rona bit hard down on her neck. With one final screech, Crystal closed her eyes.

"There. I'm on my way." Rona said, padding away as everyone froze with fear.

Mighty power… Rona… mighty power… Rona… Rona… the name… it means mighty power! Echo thought.

"NO!" He shouted, running after Rona. She was on the edge of the training cliff, about to climb down. Echo rammed hard into her back, sending her tumbling across the dirty ground. Her back was covered in dust as she reached the end of the cliff.

"THE ONE WITH MIGHTY POWER WILL BE LEFT IN THE DIRT!" He screeched, swiping her face as Rona stumbled off the cliff, falling down, down, down.

"You're dead! You're dead!" Echo announced, his body full of relief that Rona was dead, but also greif for Crystal. Was *she* really gone?

"Crystal!" Storm yelled, burying his head into her fur. "No... I love you too much to let you die...!"

Crystal's eyes opened slightly, and she tried to talk, but all Storm could hear was blood gurgling in her throat.

"Get leaves! Get leaves to cover up her throat!" Storm demanded, and Cedar nodded, quickly picking up leaves of the ground and gathering them up on her throat.

"Storm... I think I'm gonna die..." Crystal finally managed to whisper in a hoarse voice. Storm shook his head. "No you're not! What do you need? Food? Water?"

"Storm..." She said, pressing her paw against the small gray wolf's fluffy chest. "It's okay. I'll still be with you, just..."

"NO!" Storm yelled, waving his tail furiously. "You're going to live!" He said, running away to get prey from next to the den.

"Eat this!" Storm said, giving her a rat. She managed to swallow a bit of it, along with some water from the stream that Marigold squeezed out of some moss she found near the stream.

"She'll live if she can rest, I think," Grayson told Storm, who was overjoyed that Crystal would probably live.

"Crystal… just in case you live.. Can you…" Storm said quietly to the gray wolf laying down. "Be my… mate?"

Crystal nodded, raising her head a bit to touch her nose to his. "Even if you're younger than me, it's still just fine," She whispered, and then rested her head back down to go to sleep.

"Just fine…" Storm repeated.

"Just fine."

Chapter 37

"How is she?" Storm asked. He had been asking Grayson about Crystal almost every day. "Just fine. Skyler told me her bite wasn't infected anymore!"

Storm let out a sigh of relief. For days and days all he felt was nervousness for Crystal. He was so scared he could barely get simple things done, things like hunting, training, and swimming.

"She'll be ready to join the pack activities again in about two days." Grayson told Storm. "Great!" Echo responded for him, padding up to them with a rabbit dangling from his jaws. "I just hunted with Willow and Swift. We picked this up for her."

Storm dipped his head in thanks as Echo gave him the prey, and then headed into the big den to deliver it to Crystal.

She laid sprawled out in her bed, breathing almost normally, her eyes half-closed. Storm didn't know if she was asleep or not.

"Crystal?" He whispered softly. The gray wolf blinked and looked up at him. "Storm! Hello!" Crystal greeted, wriggling around to lay with her paws in front of her.

"I got you some prey…" Storm said, dropping the prey in front of her. "Well, I didn't get it, actually. Echo caught it."

"Oh, no, Storm, that's fine!" Crystal shook her head, pushing away the rabbit. "I can catch my own." She heaved out of bed, wincing, but still able to stand.

"No, Crystal. You need to rest." Storm demanded, laying his tail on her back to signal her to sit back down. She let out a quiet grumble, opening her mouth to protest, but then laying down obediently.

"Thanks for the prey," Crystal mumbled, giving him a quick lick on his cheek and then lowering her head to eat the rabbit.

"No problem!" Storm replied, licking her back and walking out of the den.

"You and Crystal, huh?" Cedar stopped him, his dark brown fur looking fluffed out angrily but his voice sounding a bit rough in it's usual way.

"Um, well…" Storm stuttered, looking away embarrassedly.

"*I* don't need a mate. I'm fine on my own!" Cedar announced, raising his head proudly. "Okay…" Storm said, turning around to go into the forest.

"I'm gonna hunt. Anyone want to come?" He yelled behind him, scanning the area. "We'll come," Tango rasped, being followed by his mother, Chestnut.

"I feel like I haven't hunted in days!" Chestnut barked, happily walking towards the smaller gray wolf with a bounce in her step. Tango followed.

"How 'bout we try near the field? I've catched some juicy rats over there." Tango suggested, pointing his paw in the direction of the field.

"But that's pretty far, and we would have to cross the stream," Storm said, shuffling his paws nervously at the thought of crossing the narrow river.

"I'd like to hunt near the field." Chestnut said softly. "You'll be okay, Storm. If you struggle then me and Tango could help you."

Pushing aside his embarrassment that Chestnut thought he would need help, Storm agreed, "Okay… we can hunt there."

"I'll go first. Or should we all go together?" Tango asked once they reached the stream, looking very confident.

"We can all go together." Chestnut said, jumping in with Tango. For a split second, Storm hesitated, his mind whirling with all the bad things that could happen. He finally forced himself to get in.

Storm could hear Chestnut and Tango paddling past him. He started to pant heavily, smacking his paws against the water as quickly as he could.

Squorsh! Storm's head ran straight into the wet grass at the other side of the narrow river. He shook his head to get the bits off and then pulled himself out, his usually fluffy dark gray fur sticking to his skin.

"Whew! We're all okay!" Chestnut said, giving her pelt a quick shake. *And all wet…* Storm thought, glancing at his soaked fur.

"Rat-faced hog!" Tango spat at what looked like nothing."A bug just bit me!"

"A bug?" Storm repeated. "I've never been bitten by a bug. They just crawl on you!"

"Nope," Tango growled, slashing the air at a skinny bug with long legs. "Swift told me Gorilla-hogs call them mosquitos. I think it's simpler to call them biters, though."

"Biters!" Chestnut rolled her eyes. "I hate those things. Such a nuisance, sucking your blood and all that."

"Sucking your *BLOOD?!*" Storm yowled. Worry filled his head again as he started slashing the air wildly. "But... but... doesn't that kill you?"

"They only get a wee bit of blood." Chestnut assured him, putting her paw on his shoulder. "It just is a little irritating. You don't feel lightheaded or anything."

"When I was small enough to fit in a gorilla- hog paw, Swift told me that one of the gorilla-hogs pups he lived with always complained about a bug with a sharp tail called a bee!" Tango exclaimed, his eyes wide.

"A sharp tail? Does it... p-poke you?" Storm stuttered nervously. "Yeah, but they don't live in forests, I think." Tango answered.

"Let's... just keep going!" Chestnut said, changing the subject. The three padded deeper into the woods. The undergrowth started to get softer, and more grass started appearing next to them.

Storm sniffed the air. It smelled fresh and plant-y.

"I heard my brother lives somewhere around here," Chestnut commented, stepping out of the forest and into the field.

Storm briefly remembered being stuck in the Gorilla hog den, and Tommy, the old dog. He wondered if Tommy was Chestnut's brother.

"Is his name Tommy?" Storm asked her. Chestnut glanced at him and shook her head. "Mint."

"MINT!" Storm repeated, gasping.

"What? Do you know where he is?"

"He's... he's..."

"Does he live in a Gorilla hog den? Is he ok?"

"Uh... I... I..."

"You? You what?"

"I don't know who M-Mint is!'

"Oh. Sorry... I yelled at you."

"It's okay..." Storm said, feeling guilty and upset for Chestnut. It would be devastating to find out if your siblings were dead. Storm pushed the thought out of his head. He would never be able to deal if his siblings died.

Chapter 38

"Rabbit." Tango whispered, his ears shooting up. Storm turned around to see a rabbit laying down on the ground in the middle of the field.

The light brown dog tiptoed carefully towards the bunny, barely even making the tall grass rustle.

"RAH!" Tango barked, jumping on the rabbit and slashing his claw against it's neck. It barely even twitched the whole entire time.

"That's weird. It didn't even hear me." Tango said, looking down at the dead bunny. "Probably 'cause you snuck up on him so well!" Chestnut commented, pressing his muzzle against her son's cheek.

"Woah!" Storm yelped. "*Great* catch, Tango!"

"No…" Tango shook his head. "It wasn't me, I know it. I think it was already dead."

"If somebody *did* already kill it, they would've taken it. It's probably just a clueless rabbit lost in it's own thoughts. Why don't you take the first bites?" Chestnut urged.

Tango hesitated, but with a quick nudge from Chestnut, he took a bite, and forced it down his throat. "It tastes awful!"

Storm stared at the remains of the rabbit. "Probably because it's all gross looking!" The rabbit's insides looked weird and messed up; like the bunny had worms or something.

"Let's hunt somewhere else!" Chestnut announced, quickly padding away.

"Two rabbits and four rats. That's pretty successful." Chestnut commented proudly, looking at all their catches.

Storm was upset Tango wasn't there. The dog had gone back to the dens early because he wasn't feeling very good. At first Chestnut was fretting about that; but Storm calmed her down by telling her everything was alright and it was probably just the rabbit, which would eventually leave his body.

"Tango is growing into a good hunter, even with a bellyache," Storm told Chestnut, carrying the two rabbits the dog had caught. Chestnut had caught two rats, and so did Storm.

"Crystal's ready to go!" Echo announced, Sky, Grayson, and Poppy following him. Storm's jaws opened wide, sending the prey in his mouth dropping to the ground.

"I thought you said she'd be ready in two days!" He gawked.

"I insisted!" Crystal squealed, padding out of the big den quickly, not even wincing a bit.

"CRYSTAL!" Storm yelled, running up to his mate and licking her wildly. "I am really glad you're okay!" Crystal smiled and nodded, but then her smile slowly turned to a frown.

"Tango isn't, though… he's really sick."

Swift popped his head out of the den. "Right now he's asleep, but I think he'll be awake in a few hours."

"Everyone should get some rest, I think," Echo said, looking up at the pinkish-orange sky. Murmurs of agree rose from the pack as they walked into the dens.

"Storm and Crystal." Poppy thought out loud. "I wonder if they'll have pups." Echo nodded slowly, shifting in his grassy bed.

"Are you upset?" Poppy asked, wrapping her tail tighter around Echo, and giving him a quick lick on his shoulder.

"I'm okay. I mean, I'm really glad. Crystal's better, Rona and Shadow are gone, Storm has finally grown up… I'm just worried about my pack, still. Leaders are always worried, right?"

Poppy licked him again. "Of course they are. It's normal. But don't worry, Tango will be okay, and so will Storm and Crystal. And Cedar, and Marigold, and everyone else! Pups mean new life, too, and new life means a bigger pack."

"Yeah. I hope they have pups." Echo said.

Almost reading his mind, Grayson barged into their den. "Crystal is expecting!"

"Are you okay? Comfortable?" Echo said. The whole pack was crowded around Crystal, even

Tango. He still felt sick, but not as sick after getting the rabbit out of his system.

"First I was stuck in this den for weeks, then I got out, and now I'm stuck in it again!" Crystal sighed, her eyes glimmering with amusement, but still a trace of annoyance.

"They're due in a month and two weeks. She was already expecting for two weeks, but nobody noticed!" Storm laughed.

Tango let out a small groan from the back of the den. Everyone shifted their head to him. He coughed and started trudging out of the den.

"I'll be right back." He grunted, tripping unsteadily through the entrance.

"He'll be okay," Poppy whispered in Echo's ear once she noticed his worried expression. "I don't know. We can't afford to lose any pack members." He quickly said back, pawing at the ground nervously.

"I wonder what they'll be," Swift thought out loud, changing the subject off Tango. Crystal let out a short yap.

"I'm not sure... but their seems like a lot in there!" Crystal rasped tiredly, wrapping her tail tight around her stomach.

"Let's give her some rest." Swift said, licking his daughter's head and turning around to snuggle back up in his and Chestnut's grass bed.

"More pups!" Echo breathed, slumping into his nest. "I'm excited." He caught Poppy's eye. They looked the same beautiful scarlet as ever; but they sparkled like stars in the sky.

"Of course you are! Everyone is!" She let out a happy quiet squeal. "I've missed having Storm running around. It's hard to believe a few days ago he was just training, and now he's a father."

A father. Echo repeated in his head, remembering when his pups were little and energetic.

So many memories swirled in his mind, it was hard for Echo to even think about an individual one. Finally it stopped on one when Cedar and Marigold were just learning to talk.

"Willow!" Echo told his pups, pointing his tail towards the light gray wolf eating prey with Swift. Cedar just squealed, and Marigold blubbered something sort of like 'Willow.'

"Swift!" Echo pointed towards the sleek black and white dog. "Swif!" Cedar repeated, with Marigold quickly saying 'Swif' after him.

"And Poppy, your mama…" He explained as the fluffy white wolf padded up to sit next to him. The pups yowled with joy at the sight of her, jumping all over her. Poppy smiled.

"And that's your father, Echo." She said, pointing her paw towards him. The pups chirped and jumped on Echo, repeating, 'fatha! Fatha!'

Father. Father.

Echo was once a father.

And now Storm would be too.

Chapter 39

"I've waited for pups way too long!" Echo sighed. "Our pups, Sky's pups, and now yours." He licked Storm's head.

"My pups." Storm murmured, his eyes wide and glittering. "I'd never thought *I* would have pups!"

"And they could be born any moment." Grayson reminded, standing up from his spot next to Skyler, and padding to Crystal.

"Are you comfortable?" He asked, laying some prey in front of her. She let out a short groan, looking up at the prey and slumping back down.

"Y-you need to eat," Storm stammered nervously, pushing the rat back towards her. Crystal nodded shortly and then forced down the prey.

"She'll be okay." Grayson reported. "Are you thirsty, Crystal?" She let out a groan and a cough.

"I think she is…" Storm said, nudging Crystal up to her feet. "Lean on me, Crystal… I'll take you to the stream."

Storm felt like he was going to collapse at any moment. Not only was he smaller then Crystal, but she weighed much more now that she was pregnant.

As she crouched down to take a sip of the stream, Crystal fell to the ground, panting quickly.

"Are you okay? Are you okay, Crystal?!" Storm asked urgently, putting his paw on her stomach. It heaved, and she let out a yowl. "It's the pups!"

It's too late to get the others. I need to deliver these pups myself. He thought, pawing at the ground nervously. "Uh-- um-" Crystal yelled again.

Her claws dug into the ground, and her legs starting flailing everywhere. Storm rested his tail on her stomach, signalling her to calm down.

Her back paws hit the floor, and she starting breathing a bit more normally, but she still was yowling.

The first pup. It was beautiful, but small. It had fluffy gray fur like Storm's, with light streaks of light gray. Her eyes were a wonderful teal. She let out a quick quiet yap.

There was one more pup; an almost white one with green eyes. Storm thought the pup's green eyes were strange, since neither him or Crystal had them.

The gray-white one was a male, and the other gray one a female.

"What are their names?" Storm asked. Crystal smiled. "Starlight and Hail,." sShe responded, her eyes glittering as she looked at her new pups.

"Are you guys- OHHHH MY GOSH." Swift stood frozen in front of them, staring at the pups in awe. Starlight let out a wail and Hail coughed.

"I'll get Grayson and the pack!" hHe squealed, running back into the depths of the forest.

"I'm a father!" Storm yelped with joy. "And I'm a mother," Crystal croaked, pulling the pups towards her.

"Noo!" Starlight squealed, wriggling out from behind her tail. Storm smirked as he looked up at Crystal. "Her first word."

"She's gonna be a feisty one!" Crystal laughed, pulling the squirming pup back towards her.

"They are so precious!" Poppy gushed, letting the pups climb all over her tail. They were about three days old now. Poppy and Crystal would watch them play for hours on end.

"Stop!" Hail squealed as Starlight flung onto him, pawing at him with her soft gray paws.

"No fun!" Starlight spat at him, stomping a few paws away from him, climbing back on Poppy's tail. Hail stuck out his tongue. Starlight did the same.

"I go on mama," Hail announced, bouncing over to Crystal. Starlight grumbled, tumbling off Poppy and onto Crystal.

"No, I go on mama! I rule mama! Get out!" She demanded, pushing Hail away. He growled. "Mama is mine!" He yowled, pouncing onto Starlight and knocking her to the ground.

"No. Bad pups! No fighting your sister, Hail!" She scooted Starlight away from Hail with her tail, placing her behind Poppy.

"They are a pawful, these two," Crystal sighed, resting her head on her paws as Starlight climbed out from behind Poppy to snuggle into Crystal's flank. Hail did the same.

"At least they'll be good fighters!" Poppy pointed out, admiring the two young wolves nestled together behind Crystal's tail.

Starlight quickly fell asleep, with Hail falling asleep quickly after her.

"How are the pups?" Tango trudged over, his tail travelling along the ground behind him. He was still sick, and for a while wasn't able to return to hunting or training.

"Great!" Poppy answered for Crystal, who added, "...at being rude to each other." Tango let out a sigh. "At least they're cute."

"How are you?" Poppy asked. Tango frowned, settling down on the ground next to them. "I don't- COUGH- feel that much better." He let out another fit of coughing, and Poppy nervously looked at Crystal.

"I'll be- COUGH- okay…" Tango assured them, coughing more after. Hail stirred a bit, wailing in his sleep.

"I'll take these two to the den," Crystal said, scooping up the pups in her jaw and padding to the big rocky cave.

Tango sighed, resting his head on his paws. "Am I ever going to be able to- COUGH- return to my duties?" He muttered, half to himself. Poppy stroked his back with her tail. "You will. Everyone always recovers!"

Tango coughed a little more. His stomach felt a bit okay; but right when that healed, he started coughing all the time. There was no way he could hunt; He'd get overwhelmed and wheezy, and his coughing would scare all the prey. If he got back to training, the same would happen; he would pant for ever.

"Always recovers…" Tango repeated. *There's a first time for everything.*

Chapter 40

"Can we train now?" Hail begged, pawing and pawing at Storm's feet. "I just need to go hunt for a bit. I promise I'll be back soon, and then I can show you a bit." Hail squealed with joy.

"I'm gonna be a better hunter *AND* a better fighter then you, Hail!" Starlight boasted, her tail waving mischievously.

"Nu-uh!" Hail yowled back, nipping her leg. Starlight yowled, shooting her back leg into Hail's face.

Hail squealed, covering his face with his paws. He opened them up squeamishly, revealing a giant scrape across his face.

"Oh my gosh," Starlight gawked. "I did that! I am such a good fighter already!"

"HAIL!" Crystal yelled, swiftly running towards the pups. She ran her paw across the scratch, her eyes wide with fear. But then, with a single glint of anger flashed in her eyes, she turned to Starlight.

"STARLIGHT!" Crystal. screamed, her eyes now completely sparkling with frustration. "I knew I shouldn't have left you alone! You will not train today, young pup!"

"What?! You're punishing me for something *GOOD?* He bit me first!" She shoved her back leg into Crystal's face, showing the ruffled bit of fur.

"And you RUINED his FACE because of that?!" behind them was a faint crying noise. Crystal whipped her head around to see Hail, his face pressed against his paws.

"My face is ruined, mama?" He sniffled. "I'm ugly now? Am I really ugly now?"

"You're never ugly, dear," Crystal licked his head, shooting a final angry glance at Starlight, who stuck out her tongue.

"I'm back!" Storm announced a few minutes later, two rats in his jaws. He looked proud at first, but then a bit nervous and jittery once he saw Starlight alone in the corner, Crystal scolding her from far away. Hail was nowhere in sight.

"Is anything w-wrong?" He stammered.

"Starlight is in big trouble. A-and…" She looked near a bush surrounding the edge of the dens.

"…Hail is hurt. He's hiding right now." Storm looked at the bush. It was wiggling a bit, as if he was re-adjusting his spot.

"What's wrong?" Storm padded up to the bush, daring to peek his head inside. Three scars wrapped across his face. They weren't bad, since they were only done by a pup, though they were noticeable.

"I'm ugly, papa! I'll never be able to fight an' hunt now! All scare off all the prey! All the wolves I'm fighting will think I'm weak!" He wailed, covering up his face.

"No, no! You are as handsome as before, Hail. And the wolves that fight you will be afraid because you look so tough! I'm getting nervous you're gonna hurt me just standing here." Storm convinced.

Hail slowly opened up his paws, revealing his face again. "You really mean it? I look tough?" Storm nodded kindly.

"Yeah!" Hail shouted in agreement. "YEAH! I'm gonna be the best wolf in the forest!" He slashed his little claws against the air.

"Tell me something I don't know!" Storm laughed, shuffling to the left so Hail could easily bounce out. "Want to get to that training?"

His eyes glittered excitedly. "Yea-yuh!" He chirped, his tail waving happily.

"Could *I* train?" Starlight asked, pushing her way passed Crystal.

"I…" Storm glanced at Crystal, who shook her head. "Next time, Starlight, promise." He forced himself to say, turning away and pretending he didn't see the sad glimmer in her eyes.

"Can we practice huntin' first?" Hail asked, glancing quickly around the forest for any prey. "The forest is so big!"

"We can hunt, but before that, I want to show you something," Storm said, pulling Hail close to him with his tail.

They padded across the flattened down grassy forest floor, trying to ignore the insects crawling all through the undergrowth. Storm heard a faint shuffle in a bush. He assumed it was a fawn; young deer scent flew into his nostrils. Hail let out an excited squee.

"This flower." Storm pointed his paw to a beautiful rose, it's petals crystallized with dew drops.

"Wow, it's really pretty!" Hail complemented, sniffing it. "And it smells really good!"

"Mmhmm. I like that it-" The loud thumping of hooves against the ground interrupted Storm. A fawn flew past them, surprising Storm so much he yowled.

Hail burst out in laughter. "You- *Hah* got scared by a.. *haha* a... *hahaha* A FAWN!" Storm sighed, licking the fur on his shoulder back down.

"Yeah, yeah, really funny. Do you wanna catch that fawn or what?" Storm asked. Hail's laughter was replaced with silent excitement as he nodded his head wildly.

"Here's the correct way to crouch. You've seen me do it." Storm lowered himself to the ground, keeping steady and balanced. Hail tried to imitate him, but was a bit unsteady. Storm nudged his flank to keep him balanced.

"Then, you pounce!" He yelled, but immediately realising he sounded *too* enthusiastic, and looked down at his paws embarrassedly.

"Pounce!" Hail repeated, shaking his back legs, and then propelling up in the air, only to be brought back down hard on the ground, a cloud of dirt puffing up into the air.

"Oof!" He squeaked as his belly hit the ground, his paws falling down ungracefully. Storm hold back laughter, shaking his head slowly.

"No, like this." Storm exclaimed, lunging up in the air again, but landing with his paws on the ground instead of his stomach.

"Woah!" Hail shouted in awe. "Where'd ya learn that?"

"Actually, your mama taught me," Storm told the little white-ish gray pup. He let out a quick yelp in surprise. "She was a great trainor. The best. And then, she ended up being my mate. It… was a dream come true." His eyes sparkled briefly as he stared into the sky, but then quickly flicked back to normal.

"N-now lets try those moves out on that darn fawn!" He said. Hail smiled. "You mean I'm ready." Storm looked his son in the eye, nodding kindly. Hail's smile grew wider.

"Nnngh…" Hail grunted, his flanks waving. The fawn was clearly in front of him; as clueless as a rock, chewing on some berries.

"RAH!" He plunged into the deer, giving it a swift scratch on it's stomach. It fell to the ground, letting out a wail.

"I'll help!" Storm growled, jumping onto the deer and biting it's neck, killing it quickly.

"My first prey!!" Hail chirped, dancing around the fawn.

"Let's bring it back to camp. Tango will be happy with it! And, you need a rest," Storm said, looking down at the deer.

Hail crouched down, picking up the deer in his jaws, but staggering under the weight and falling down.

"I got it," Storm said, hoisting the fawn up onto his back. Hail nodded, looking straight forward, his head held high and his eyes sparkling with pride.

Chapter 41

"A fawn? A whole *fawn?*" Starlight spat, her eyes flashing with anger. "And while you were catching that I was sitting here, doing nothing?"

She spun her head around to face Crystal.

"I... *HATE* you!" she screamed.

Starlight spun back around, barrelling into the forest. Hail dropped the fawn onto the ground.

"Starlight!" Echo ran out of the spot he was sitting, following the gray pup. He heard her snarl in anger from a little ahead of him.

"Starlight..." Echo skidded ahead of Starlight, blocking her path to run. The anger in her eyes slowly faded as she stared at him.

"W-walk with me," He whispered, stepping to the side for her to go next to him.

"You don't like life in the pack so far, ey?" Echo asked, his feet crunching against leaves on the ground. He looked up at the dull clouds sprawled across the gray sky. It was obvious a storm was on its way.

Starlight shrugged. "Everyone blames me for everything! I mean, I *guess* I have a bad temper, but that's because everyone's so ANNOYING!"

Echo was actually a bit surprised by the pup. Other pups would act nervous around and really want to impress their Alpha, but Starlight was quite the opposite.

"Maybe if you changed they would too," Echo told her, but immediately regretted it and wished to take back his words. It's rude to ask someone to change, right?

Surprising him again, Starlight started to slowly nod. "Maybe you're right..." She muttered, a trace of anger in her voice.

"I'm always right," Echo joked, nudging her playfully. The pup giggled in laughter, pouncing onto Echo.

"Hey, hey, hey now..." He stood up, sending Starlight tumbling across the ground. "That's not proper fighting! Let's teach you some real good moves." She brightened.

"You guys took g forever!" Hail exclaimed, his eyes wide and curious. Starlight's face darkened with mischievousness. "Echo fell in the stream and I saved hiiim!" sShe lied.

"I didn't fall in the stream!" Echo waved his tail with fake-anger. Starlight laughed.

"No, we practiced hunting moves. Wanna see?" Starlight asked, bouncing over to her brother. He nodded happily.

Echo watched the pups talk and train. It was hard to believe just an hour ago they were enemies.

"Starlight!" Crystal huffed, stepping out angrily of the big den. But before she could reach the grey pup, Storm stopped her with his tail.

She made a small *oof* sound, and gave Storm a questionable glance.

"They're fine," Storm calmed Crystal, licking her ruffled fur down. "But what if she doesn't learn?"

"She will. It was an accident, anyway."

Crystal sat down, her furiousness fading away. She watched her pups play for a bit, but noticed the sky getting darker.

Hail looked up at the sky. "Night already? Hmm!" Starlight shook her head. "It's the middle of the day!"

"It's the storm that was coming." Echo told the pups. "Storm? Like dada?" Starlight asked, looking back up at the cloudy sky.

"Storm is another word for when there's extreme weather, like snow or rain," Echo answered. The pup's eyes shined. "Snow? Rain?" They repeated confusedly.

"You'll see," Crystal walked in, licking their heads.

"Can we pleeease go out now, mama?" Hail begged. They had been in the den for a long time now, waiting for the snowstorm to calm down.

"I suppose. I'll have to watch you, though." Crystal padded over to her excited pups bouncing cheerfully out of the den.

"Snow!" The pups stared in awe at the crystally drops spiralling down to the ground. Starlight pounced in, sending a cloud of the powdery snow into the air. Hail's scruffy fur collected all the snow, leaving him looking like he was made of snow.

"This is so cool!" Starlight squeaked, spinning around. Hail swung his paw into the snow, sending up another huge puff of snow, which fell down onto Starlight. She laughed and sneezed as the snow tickled her nose.

"Oh my gosh!" Starlight's ears perked up in surprise. "You could-" She paused, scooping up snow in her paws. Starlight threw the snow into Hail's face. "-throw 'em!"

"Why I oughta!" Hail growled, whipping his tail around to make snow spray in her face.

The pups broke out into a huge game of 'throw the snow,' as the senior wolves and dogs laughed.

Once the snow finally stopped, it was dark out. The pups snuggled into bed with Crystal and Storm, Grayson was led into bed by Skyler, Swift and Chestnut slept together, Tango, alone in the corner, keeping quiet but coughing. Willow sat with Boulder, quietly telling him stories. Marigold slept next to Cedar. Echo was sitting next to Poppy, who was snoring rhythmically.

Echo was tired, but not that tired. Sleep couldn't find him; for he was too excited, even for nothing, and too happy, even for nothing. He had done what he dreamed to do, build a pack. And it was his own pack. Echo's pack.

Chapter 42

"Summer! It feels like we've been waiting forever!" The pack followed after Echo, their tails waving happily. The seniors were in the front; Chestnut, Swift, Willow, Poppy, Grayson, Skyler and Echo. The younger wolves followed; Tango, Crystal, Cedar, Marigold and Storm. Finally, the pups followed, Hail, Starlight, and Boulder.

They had all agreed to take a walk, look at their territory. Even Tango agreed, despite his cough, which had actually gotten worse. Now he usually hung out with Grayson and Sky, collecting useful plants or flowers.

Echo could sense the wolves were getting tired by the way they let out little groans randomly, and would occasionally trip on a rock.

"Let's take a rest," he announced, settling down.

The wolves and dogs sat in silence for a bit, looking around at their friends. Finally, Willow spoke up. "Well…" He hesitated. "I bet you'd all be wondering about my backstory. I've been in this pack for a while. I think it's time."

The pack's ears perked up curiously. They had all been waiting for this moment, and were excited out of their mind.

"When I was born, my mother immediately left the next day. I didn't know why, but soon found out that it was because she was angry at my dad. My dad taught me a lot. His name was… Flame…

because he was the color of ash. Dark, dark gray. My mom was light gray, I think. Her name was... umm... sapphire." He paused, shuffling his paws.

"My dad taught me lots- more then even any of you would teach Hail or Starlight or Boulder." He flicked his tail towards the pups.

"That's why I was sort of... acting... *smart* around you when you saved me, Echo." Willow told him.

"Anyway, we practiced so much- *so much*- until one day, he just..." He gulped. "He said he was going hunting, and he did. But after a while, he wasn't back, so I went to investigate. And I found blood... his blood... on the ground, along with bear scent. A bear must've wandered off from the Gorilla-Hog forest and came to our remote forest."

He looked down at his paws quickly and then back up at his pack. "I didn't know what to do, so I just walked for a while, and ended up near the stream. And... well, you know what happens next."

"Oh, Willow- I, I'm sorry! Your life must've been so hard... I feel really bad." Echo apologized, licked Willow's shoulder. But, Willow shook his head.

"Don't apologize. You saved my life. And brought me to this wonderful pack. I couldn't ask for anything more, Echo."

The whole pack 'aaaawwww'ed as Echo stared gratefully at Echo, and once they were done, he lunged over to frantically lick the gray wolf's head.

"I am so, so, SO happy all of you make up my pack. You guys are just… incredibly amazing!" Echo announced once he had finally had enough of licking Willow.

For the rest of the day, the pack ate and ate, talked and talked, laughed and laughed. It was probably the best day of Echo's life; maybe even better than the day he met Willow.

Once the sun started setting, and the sky started to turn pink-orange, the pack soon decided to go back to the dens.

Echo turned around to go with them, but something held him back. He looked back to see Willow, sitting alone, looking at the sun falling down under the horizon. It was a perfect view, right on the cliff, where you could see everything.

Echo padded up to sit next to Willow. Willow gave Echo a nice glance and then looked back at the sunset.

"I love summer sunsets," Echo commented, scanning the sky. "Cheesy…" Willow murmured jokingly.

"WILLOW!" Echo laughed, flicking him with his tail.

"It's true! I'll we've been talking about is cheesy stuff." Willow replied, a fake-sinister, amused gleam in his eyes.

Echo didn't reply. He stared at Willow, a big smile across his face, his eyebrows hunched.

"It's okay, I like cheesy!" Willow calmed him, jumping onto his paws. Echo shook his head. "Silly!"

The wolves broke out in a play-fight. For the first time ever since the pack had started, Echo didn't feel embarrassed about acting like a pup.

A pup... Echo thought as he felt Willow pouncing on him. *I remember when Willow was a pup. He was so scrawny, so helpless... but now, he's full-grown, a great wolf, a loyal wolf... a friend.*

"Whew!" Echo got up, propelling Willow across the ground. "You're lucky you're such a fat furball, Echo! All you have to do is stand and you'll beat your opponents!" Willow said.

There was a moment of silence.

"KIDDING!" Willow assured him, pouncing again. After a few minutes of play-fighting and laughing and fake-insulting, they headed back.

The walk felt like the exact same walk when Echo had just saved Willow from the stream. When they were walking in silence; Echo glancing at Willow every few seconds. Things were so different now. So, so different.

Rona was gone. Shadow was gone. Chee was gone.

Echo wasn't a big, fat furball.

Echo had a purpose.

Echo had a pack.

-The end-

About the Authors

Sara Rydstrom and Natalie Merendino

Are the creators of this book! Sara was the author who wrote the beginning, middle, and end, and came up with many plot twists, new characters, and even some problems! Natalie was the amazing co-author of the book who helped with ideas, characters' personalities, and also some problems! They both had a lot of fun writing this book for 20 time, and all profits made will go to a wolf sanctuary.